The author is a late starter who only began to write short stories five years ago. He began his writing career by writing tribute poems for family and friends to celebrate birthdays, weddings and special occasions. He then decided to try his hand at writing short stories by attending creative writing classes and joining a U3A writing group. He has built a portfolio of a range of stories that covers many genres, including humour, and human and social attitude tales inspired in Glasgow.

I would like to dedicate this effort to my wife, Janice, and children, Lisa and Martin, who have supported me throughout, as well as my sisters and brother.

William Brown

TWICE LAST NIGHT

AUSTIN MACAULEY PUBLISHERS™
LONDON · CAMBRIDGE · NEW YORK · SHARJAH

A CIP catalogue record for this title is available from the British Library.

ISBN 9781528973519 (Paperback)
ISBN 9781528973533 (ePub e-book)

www.austinmacauley.com

First Published (2021)
Austin Macauley Publishers Ltd
25 Canada Square
Canary Wharf
London
E14 5LQ

I would like to acknowledge the support of my colleague Alison Clark and members of U3A, particularly Irene Conway, who helped build up my confidence as a writer.

Wanted – Alive and Kicking

Shirley and the other members of the Alive & Kicking troupe were rehearsing the lines for a forthcoming performance. The atmosphere in the community centre was joyous as the septuagenarian singers, also known as the Red Road Young Uns, waited to find out which role the director had allocated to them for the next show. Most were hoping they had no lines to remember, it was too difficult to learn at their ages, and hoped they could just sing. The meeting was interrupted by the project manager who wanted to introduce them to a new member who wanted to join the group.

"Hi, everyone," said Eulelia cheerfully, "meet Charlie, who is joining us. I know you will all make him feel most welcome. I'll leave you to make your own introductions. Good luck, Charlie, I'm sure you will have a great time here."

Shirley nearly fell off her stool. She was Charlie's ex-wife. She married him when she was 18, lived with him for 27 years and hadn't seen him in 27 years since he left her to go and work in Corby and never returned. She was in shock. She excused herself and immediately went to Eulelia's office along the corridor from the hall.

"You can't let him join, Eulelia, he's my ex. I don't want anybody to know my business here. I was here first – please tell him that he will have to go!"

"Oh my God, Shirley, I had no idea. Didn't even know you had been married. I understand the way you feel but I can't just tell him to leave. He is just here and he seems like a nice man. Why don't you see how it goes? And if it gets too uncomfortable, we'll see what compromise we can come up with. Please, don't you leave, Shirley, you have made so many good friends here and you're a valued member of the cast. Please think of what I am saying to you?"

Shirley was naturally upset but after composing her thoughts, she decided to take Eulelia's advice, after all a lot of water had flowed under the bridge and she really had moved on. She had never met anyone else, nor had she any desire to. Her break up was a long time ago, her tears had dried up. She put on a little makeup and went back into the hall. Charlie acknowledged her immediately. He nodded and waited on a response. She grinned back grudgingly.

"Long time, no see. How are you?"

"Fine, thanks. What are you doing back in Glasgow?"

"Just wanted to come home. Look! Sorry about everything before. Do you want me to go away? I will if you want!"

"No, don't go on my account. Let's just see how it goes."

The rest of the gang were oblivious to any feelings of resentment or regret. Shirley and Charlie were very discreet and carried on treating each other with the utmost dignity and respect. Their marriage was over long before it was officially terminated. The pressures arising from a childless marriage in those days were too much for them to bear. The director began to distribute the script for the new show. To everyone's delight, the only speaking part was given to the show presenter and he could read from a script. Everyone familiarised themselves with their songs, no one was objecting. They had six weeks to get it right. After a short period of discussion over a few glasses of wine, they decided to have a wee singsong in the hall. They all wanted to hear Charlie sing first – to gauge the competition.

Charlie stood up and belted out, "Tootsie, Tootsie, goodbye, Tootsie, Tootsie, don't cry."

Shirley was next, "You made me love you, I didn't want to do it."

The crowd egged them on to do a duet. Shirley declined. She began to think about all the house parties they used to have. They did often sing together. The parties were nearly always at their house as they were DINKYS (double income

10

no kids yet). They did have some good times, she pondered. Other cast members all did their turn and then it was time to leave the club.

"Fancy a drink, just for old times' sake?" chanced Charlie.

"Why not?" Shirley said. She really wanted to know where he had been, what his life was and why he had returned to Scotland. They went to their local Weatherspoon's for a bite to eat and a couple of drinks. It was like a first date.

It was strange. There were no gaps in the conversation as though their 27-year-old hiatus had never happened. She was surprisingly comfortable with him as he explained that he had never met anyone either, nor had he wanted to really. He explained that all he really wanted was a family, and when that never happened, he thought the grass might be greener elsewhere. He admitted he was wrong. He regretted ever leaving her. He was retired now and realised that he never really had anything to keep him in Corby. He had decided to return to Glasgow. He explained that he did not know she was in Alive & Kicking. She told him that her story was very similar to his. All she wanted was for him to try to find out why it never happened, but he was always too embarrassed to go to the doctor. She had never been able to trust another man. She joined the club for company and was grateful for it.

They agreed to let bygones be bygones, for now.

Over the next few weeks and months, Charlie became a regular at the club. He was very popular. He was always chirpy, generous with his praise for others and most of all, he could sing. As you know in Glasgow, good singers are rated more highly than good doctors, especially on a Saturday karaoke night.

Charlie and Shirley continued to see each other surreptitiously. No one in the club knew but some did suspect something was going on. The dates were becoming less strained and more cordial, if not quite passionate. Their conversation was full of reminiscences, catching up with the whereabouts of their old friends and neighbours etc. Shirley knew all the answers, so she did most of the talking. Finally, after a few drinks, Shirley asked a question of her own:

"Charlie, please tell me honestly what made you go – was it me?"

"No!" Charlie said apologetically, "I left to try to help you to get on with your life and maybe meet someone who could give you what I couldn't."

He went on, "Do you know the straw that broke the camel's back? Do you know what they used to call me in the shipyard at Govan? It wasn't Charlie the Gaffer, it was Charlie the Jaffa! Sad isn't it."

The rehearsals and dates continued and the couple became closer but not yet intimate. Shirley's distrust of men persisted although she quite clearly had feelings for her ex-husband. She knew that deep down he was a good guy, but he had let her down ever so badly. There was, however, another issue which kind of forced her hand. During the rehearsals, one of the members of the troupe, Iris Armour, had started to overtly flirt with Charlie. Well! He was after all, as far as they knew, single, charming, fun, funny and he could sing. Iris, apart from her smooth singing voice, was well-known for her promiscuity. She wasn't known as yo-yo knickers for no reason. She had a legendary tattoo on her ankles which declared, 'Heavens Above'. She had tried it on with several members to see if they were still alive and kicking.

She said half-jokingly, "C'mon over to my place tonight, Charlie, I'll have nothing on but the radio!"

"I'd love to, darling, but I'm washing my hair. You're gonna have to have Sky TV and offer a hearty breakfast to get me round," Charlie retorted.

Charlie was playing a blinder, balancing between showing a slight interest in Iris, whilst if there was any chance, proclaiming that his main desire was to reconnect with his wife.

Finally, Shirley cracked. She gave way to her emotions. She invited Charlie over for dinner at her house. He did his first sleepover that very night. She proposed that Charlie move in to see how it would work. It had taken her months to get over her pride and sense of failure, but she realised that Charlie had been her past and would now be her future. She wanted to be with him in her twilight years. The living arrangements went as successfully as their showbiz careers. They ended up as a double act on stage at the next show, performing *Islands in the Stream*. They were once again prepared to tell the world that they were an item.

Once the dust had settled and their co-habitation was permanent, Charlie phoned the pension service to let them know that they were once again a couple:

The voice at the other end of the phone enquired as to when they were reconciled?

Charlie cheekily replied, "Twice last night and once this morning."

They were indeed once again alive and kicking.

A Place in History

I remember the first time I met Patrick Potion. He was standing at the bar in the Rowallan Bar. It was a Sunday afternoon. The bar had been full of fans watching a football match, but was now beginning to empty as Celtic had lost and there was no real reason to stay and celebrate a defeat. He was standing on his own, as was I. I had gone to the pub with my brother but he had gone home. He struck up a conversation about football and the bar service or the lack of it. His face was familiar to me as I had seen him in the bar with another group of regulars, so I was comfortable in conversation.

It's that kind of bar where even if you had never spoken directly with someone, you knew someone who had; there was a sort of common bond with all the drinkers and staff, probably to do with the football.

During the course of our discussion, it turned out that we both had a lot of mutual friends. Patrick was a former member of a writing club called 'The Eastwood Writers', and I was a current member of the club. I told him I was a novice writer but that I was enjoying myself making up poems, and now I was trying to develop my skills into writing short stories. Patrick told me that he had been writing for years, but had given up as he had never managed to get any of his work published. I encouraged him to start again. I told him just to treat it as a hobby and not to judge success in terms of publication. I recognised that this idea was not compatible with Patrick's way of thinking. He was competitive. He was materialistic and he would only invest time in something if there was something in it for him. However, we continued our blethering about our reading preferences. Then, I realised that I had stayed out longer than intended, and said cheerio hurriedly. I knew we would talk again if we met, and that's what happened as a close friendship grew.

We used to meet once a week in the 'Poet's Corner' of the bar to talk about new stuff we had written. It was called 'Poet's Corner' because apparently years ago, there used to be a group of writers from Thornliebank, who used to spend their time writing rhymes and stories in the corner of the bar. The guys involved were all well-known local guys who passed commentary on anything or anybody of interest in the village and beyond. None of the writers had anything published, but they were all still celebrities in that bar. The older regulars all knew them personally, of course, the bar had completely changed and there was no place in today's world for that type of culture. Their place had been taken over by the pool table and the fruit machine. The great thing was that I had teamed up with someone who had the same interest in writing as me, he had resurrected his writing career and I didn't feel like so much of a woos as I previously felt as an isolated, solitary writer in Thornliebank. I never really felt part of the writers' group at Eastwood as those nice people were all a bit twee for me. Patrick wasn't like that at all. He was down to earth and could write humorously about all matters topical and political.

Patrick and I continued to meet socially and used to pass the time showing each other the work we had written. Patrick was becoming a frustrated writer because he was desperate to have his work seen, appreciated and published. We bought that year's *Artists and Writers Handbook*. I continued to write mainly for fun, but also to give poems to people who were celebrating special occasions like birthdays, retirements, new jobs and sometimes just to take the piss out of people who were taking themselves too seriously. Patrick was spending his time writing to prospective publishers and agents to see if anyone wanted to see his work. It was proving to be a fruitless exercise as he was rebuffed time and time again.

Then, I persuaded him to join me in doing a creative writing course at Glasgow University. It was only £63 pounds for ten lessons and I thought it might help us both identify if we had any talent, or maybe even give us some ideas on what to write about. We both enrolled in the course.

The course was good fun. It was great to know there were many others who shared your hobby. The tutor, an American girl with lots of letters after her name, was so enthusiastic and obviously loved what she was doing. The class was a mix of personalities, but Mrs Parrott dominated it. I liked her because you never felt she was sitting on your shoulder and she was innovative. Apart from the course, Patrick and I continued to see each other. Two things happened that changed both our lives and our friendship forever. The first thing was that my wife happened to say to our next-door neighbour that I was doing this creative writing course when Ann told her that her father, Andrew Brand, used to write poetry, and was one of the original poets who used to inhabit Poet's Corner in the Rowallan. Ann brought in her dad's poetry for me to see. It was fantastic, breathtakingly funny, original and unique. I couldn't wait to tell Patrick about it and asked Ann if I could show it. The work was so good, it deserved to be read out loud. I showed Patrick the work and he too was as amazed as I was. We spent ages reading it and talking about it. Around about the same time, I was beginning to write more topical poetry and I penned a poem in support of the Glasgow 2014 Commonwealth Games bid. Like always, I shared my words and thoughts with Patrick. He really liked this poem, which went something like this:

THE GAMES

Won't it be great for Glasgow's esteem,
Hosting those games in two thousand and fourteen,
Filling those peripheral housing schemes,
Crammed with international athletic teams.

Our kids can look forward to so much fun,
And learn to hop, skip and run,
Giving them the motivation to take to the pedal,
In the hope of winning a Commonwealth gold medal.

We are ready to send our invitations,
To the Africans, the Aussies and the Asians,
We have delivered the plan, give them your support,
Built the pools, the tracks, the grids for the sports.

Can we leave behind the drugs and abuse?
The records show our health needs a boost,
Let's move away from our bad news,
Let's enjoy those brand-new venues.

A few weeks later, however, I began to detect a difference in Patrick's attitude towards me in the bar. When he came in, he didn't join me as usual – just a nod or a wave – but not a real conversation. I began to think I had offended him in some way. I couldn't for the life of me think was what wrong with him. Eventually, I confronted him but he never really offered any explanation for his cold behaviour. He said he was holidaying from writing and had nothing of interest to show, so I left it at that.

Later, I found out that Patrick was going away on a promotional tour with the Glasgow 2014 team. He had taken it upon himself to forward my poem to the marketing team who obviously felt it was a great reflection of the way Glaswegians felt about their town being a candidate city for this important multi-national event. He had omitted to tell them that he hadn't written the poem, instead he took the kudos and the fees all for himself. The poem was all over their literature, on their website – it was everywhere with his name on it. Now the fly bastard was off to Melbourne, Toronto, Delhi, Singapore and Lagos on an all-expenses paid trip sponsored by the city fathers. I was livid when I found out what was happening, but I couldn't do anything about it. How could I prove that I had written this poem? I was bitter and bitterness festers. How could a so-called friend do this to me?

For Patrick, the window of opportunity had opened. He grasped his chance for fame and fortune with both hands. Loath Press, who were a firm who had turned him down before, but now saw an opportunity for themselves to cash in on his newfound fame, gave him a publishing contract. Patrick used his people skills to the full in order to get himself known within the literary community around the city, and he worked tirelessly to promote his first book of poems called *Odes by the Common Glasgow Man*. His book was very well received and reviewed. He was becoming very well known for his ability to write funny rhymes on topical subjects. The horrible thing was when you looked at the titles in his anthology – none of the poems were actually written by him. Each poem in the selection was either written by me or my fellow poet, Andrew Brand, who had died a long time ago.

This little runt (that's rhyming slang) appeared first on Radio Clyde 2 *Book Programme*, then it was the *Fred MacAulay Show* on Radio Scotland with Gloria Hunniford. His book sold thousands of copies – very similar impact to that shared with Pam Ayres in the 1970s. He was on Scottish News, *Offside with Tam Cowan* and ended up as a celebrity guest on *Parkinson* and the *Frank Skinner Show*. Patrick had moved up in the world and no longer lived in Thornliebank. He had bought a pad in Newton Mearns. I, on the other hand, had stopped writing altogether, sickened and blocked. I was a drunk who nobody believed. I felt like the fifth Beatle. I was still doing my day job and felt incensed anytime I heard of him or saw anything of him. He was busy doing the after-dinner circuit.

I needed revenge. I did not know how to get it, and then I had a stroke of luck. Ann, who was still my next-door neighbour, had gone to America to visit her sister. She told her sister the story of Patrick Potion, who was now the machair of Scotland, and she contacted me. Nancy told me that she had registered her father's work and had copyright to it all. She filled me in with all the details and told me to go to a lawyer to pursue Patrick for breach of copyright. I contacted Fiona Parrott, the university lecturer, who told me all about copyright and the legalities involved. I then approached my lawyer and asked him to prosecute the case against this phoney parasite who had stolen the soul of a dead poet and the livelihood of a living one. Patrick denied all the accusations put before him. He claimed he had written every line of work on his own. However, I was able to provide the manuscripts that I had written for all my pieces and Ann was able to provide all her father's notes and typing and copyright details. Patrick was goosed and he knew it. He offered a settlement to prevent the matter going to court, but I refused. I wanted my day. All the witnesses turned up and Patrick was shown up for what he was – an absolute fraud, a shameless thief and an honourless friend.

I was awarded a huge sum of money in compensation, but nothing could really make up for the loss of the pleasure destroyed when I could no longer write and the loss of faith in humanity. He stole my place and Andrew Brand's place in the history of Glasgow.

Badness

All the signs were there from when he was a small child. You know the type – crying loudly till he got his own way, biting other children in nursery, pulling the legs off spiders, frightening sleeping animals with fireworks, excessive temper-tantrums, disruptive behaviour from P1 onwards, throwing furniture at teachers, bullying, expelled from school at ten, stealing, vandalising property, harassing neighbours, terrorising siblings and steadily progressive criminal behaviour before he was finally incarcerated at Glenochil Young Offenders Institution, where he learned even more deviant tricks. Charlie always looked after number one and cared not a jot for anyone else. Nowadays, his behaviour would be treated as a disorder, but back then he was just an uncontrollable child who would not obey.

On his release from his YOI, he vowed he would never be caught up with again. He immediately made a beeline for his mother's house. She was surprised to see him and wouldn't have, but he needed cash quickly to buy some decent clothes. He stole money from her purse and headed into town and spent it all on a suit, shirts, shoes and a haircut.

Having smartened himself up, that very night he ventured into his local bar, The Royal Oak. Even at his young age, he had accrued the reputation of being a madman, so most people gave him a wide berth and avoided eye contact. He surveyed the scene. Nothing much had changed since he was last in, six months ago. There was a disco blaring in the lounge. He thought he'd go in and try his luck – there were loads of young girls drunk and dancing.

On that night, he met Louise, a mouse of a girl, who worked in a local knitwear factory stitching knickers for a living. She must have been the only person on the premises who did not know him. Charlie produced an uncharacteristically charm offensive performance. Louise was hooked. She seemed to enjoy the thrill of entertaining the local bad boy. She listened intently to his stories of how he had battered this one and that one. Somehow, she felt protected. Within months, he had turned that wee mouse into a monster, who was capable of the same amount of violence and depravity that he was. He introduced her to cannabis and smack. In no time, she was addicted to the drugs as she was to his lifestyle. He controlled her. He brutalised her. He would not let any of her family near her. He even brutalised his dog and his children when they eventually were old enough. Together, they administered the drug, money lending and credit card scams in the scheme where they lived. People were too terrified to do anything against this Bonnie and Clyde duo, and with good reason.

Louise and Charlie used suppliers from Liverpool and London. They used a network of couriers usually hooked or in debt to them. They used to obtain fake IDs and con landlords into renting them property, which would then be used to obtain credit cards and bank loans and hire purchase goods. They used to leave a trail of debt and destruction behind them, then move on. They were both very good actors. They made up a story about not being able to pay a deposit to all the landlords because they were saving up for IVF treatment as they had used up their free goes, and were desperate to start a family. At least, four homeowners were taken in with that one. They thought that this was funny because in reality they already had three kids. The usual sequence of events was that they were long gone before the landlords and the stores who had been conned, caught up with them.

They were building up capital but, far worse, they were building up reputation for being the cruellest and heartless bastards in Scotland. Strangely enough, Charlie was not particularly entrepreneurial. All he wanted was to control his little patch. This kept the big boys – the real gangsters – away, and my, what a job he made of terrorising the whole of the scheme. Louise was every bit as bad. Her main role was to intimidate wives and partners of those who owed money or who hadn't paid their drug debt. She usually did this down at the school gate. She was a moll. She could often be seen dragging some young girl by the hair down the street. She did not take prisoners and her violence often extended into prolonged torture as she laid into anyone who crossed her path, or whose children had upset her children in any way. She was vicious. She took her lead from her crooked partner.

Their reign of terror seemed endless. The beatings they doled out mercilessly and with regularity. No one ever dreamed of informing the authorities for fear of severe reprisals. It was not long before he took over the local pub. He had no interest in the spirit trade. He just employed people to run it and used it as an office for issuing his goods. The only time he was seen in the bar was when he was after someone. The unfortunate victim was usually dragged out screaming for mercy but none was ever given. These public displays kept order. One time, there was a disturbance in the pub when the barman refused to serve a drunken teenager any more drink. The young man foolishly picked up a bar stool and launched it at the gantry, breaking the mirror and some bottles of spirits. The staff did not react but the young boy was advised to leave quickly. The next week, the boy was severely battered as he came off the Rangers supporters' bus in the middle of the main street. Charlie was well able to pay henchman to carry out his seriously dirty work. No witnesses came forward and Charlie was visible in the bar at the time of the incident. Yet, another unreported crime and another life ruined. Charlie's response in breaking a mirror was certainly seven years bad luck in this case.

One time, he had a rival in the scheme; however, this rivalry was fairly temporary. This man, Jamie, was a violent ex-con had just been released from Barlinnie, having completed his sentence for murdering someone in Govan. He, as was his nature, wanted to set out some markers and make his presence felt. He, too, was a vicious, liberty-taking bastard who picked on vulnerable defenceless victims. The inevitable show down came. It took place in a public arena, like an amphitheatre, curtains twitched, lights were turned off and the onlookers anticipated a bloody battle. They were not disappointed. Charlie stood at the bottom of the stairwell armed with a baseball bat. He baited and provoked his rival with insults and threats. Jamie came down the stairs carrying a huge machete. They circled each other, Jamie lost his footing on the wet grass. It was all over in minutes. Charlie rendered him unconscious by battering him over the skull with the bat. He then proceeded to boot him in the ribs and genitals. Jamie whimpered. He was left almost for dead. His wife came out of her house to help him, but Louise then set about her too. The victorious couple left the square. The losers left the scheme in stealth, never to return.

The vicious cycle continued as Charlie dominated life in the village with impunity. He once forced a customer, who owed him money, to sell his house to him to repay his debt. Robin borrowed £500 from him in January 2012 and by June, found that he now owed £15,000. Charlie took his house for the debt, started it up and resold it for £75,000. Nice work for £500.

His demise came about rather innocuously and unexpectedly. One day, he was standing in the square where a lot of business was conducted. It was unusually quiet. He was on his own. He usually had his German shepherd with him. There was a young woman walking towards him trying to avoid eye contact.

"What you looking at, ya fucking cow?" he said aggressively.

The girl did not reply but just scurried up into her close. When she arrived home, she told her husband what had just happened. He was in rage.

"Right, that's it. I am going get that bastard. Talking to you like that!"

Despite her pleas for him to ignore him, he stealthily opened his door. He stood in the close. He was waiting for the right moment. Charlie turned his back to the close front.

Danny quite calmly battered his baseball bat over the top of his head. He was down and Danny rained kicks and punches on him as he was overcome with anger. Charlie's crown of invincibility had all at once been removed. The young couple fled the scheme. Neighbours who had seen what happened, went to see if he was still alive. He was, barely. An ambulance was tailed as he was admitted to hospital with a fractured skull, ruptured spleen and severe damage to his spine. No one witnessed the incident. He never really recovered. In fact, that was a black day for him because while he was away, Louise took her opportunity to escape with their five children.

Louise went to a woman's refuge and got help, which transformed her life. She went into a rehabilitation centre and her addiction to cocaine was cured. She left him for good. Her children have somehow survived. Charlie is now like an old man, bent over and hunched. He still has a horrible temperament, so bad that Cordia will not send any carers to him, and the Samaritans won't return his calls.

Ben Gold

Ben Gold was well named, for everything that he touched seemed to turn to gold. Not that he was born with a silver spoon, in fact, he was one of twelve children from a Russian family who had escaped from the pogroms. He and his sister, Rosie, were born in Leeds, England, but his other ten siblings were brought over from the Baltics. He was born in 1900. His parents arrived with nothing and left the north of England with nothing, to move to Glasgow to be nearer relatives in 1904. Ben and his sister were actually thought of as miracle babies because his mother gave birth when she was well into her forties, which was almost the same age as life expectancy in the slums of England in those times. Ben's family were from a Jewish tribe known as Ashkenazi renowned for their creativity and entrepreneurship even within their own larger community, and Ben was stereotypical.

The family moved to an area in Glasgow called the Briggait, near the Gorbals, where a large Yiddish community was settled. The family lived in a large one-roomed tenement with an outside-shared toilet. Everyone could whistle (so avoiding lavatory embarrassments). They were so poor that they actually took in two lodgers to help to pay the rent. Ben was different from the rest of the family. There was something special about him. He was the type of small boy everyone loved. He was charismatic and could charm the birds out of trees. As a young lad, he showed the type of determination to succeed, often found within people who immigrated to another country. He was born here but still had more of the ambition and drive to improve his quality of life.

As young as ten, he started to sell old clothes and bric-a-brac in the Briggait market. He learned how to buy and sell, he mastered customer service and developed a line of pattoir, which endeared him to the other traders and to the people who used the market. Ben had vision. He saved up his profits and then rented a stall in the Barras market in Glasgow, selling tools. During the week, he used to scour the west of Scotland to look for second-hand tools and then he sold them at the weekend in his stall. He quickly became really well known by all the tradesmen in the area. He used to speak to them all to establish his clientele, to find out what equipment they needed and then he would source it out for them and sell it to them at a profit.

When the time was right, Ben expanded his business and bought a shop, selling and hiring tools in Glasgow High St. The shop was proudly called 'Ben's Tool Shop'. He knew everyone who was anyone in Glasgow. He was only in his early twenties, but he had built a reputation as a good, honest, kind trader who would go out of his way to help his customers. Even if they could not afford their tools, he would let them pay.

As ever, Ben had an eye for the pound and the vision and entrepreneurship to make it happen. He could see that Glaswegian punters liked a bet, so, he and his new partner and friend, Jackie Sheva, started an illegal bookmaker business in the back of the tool shop. Ben became really wealthy, very quickly as bookmakers often did. It was a double-whammy win-win situation, central location, well-known business, frequented by the gambling fraternity (workies) and a trusted partner. The shop was a goldmine.

Socially, Ben was being urged by his parents to settle down and get married. He was betrothed to his cousin, Annie, who was his mother's sister's daughter. He was a reluctant groom but a loyal son, who would not have gone against his parent wishes. It was fairly common within the Jewish sector for marriages to be arranged. He married Annie. She was attractive but also eccentric. She had an unusually vitriolic temperament but a heart of gold. In today's terms, she had mental health issues, but then she was considered to be fragile.

Ben's businesses continued to thrive. He and Annie lived in a sumptuous five-bedroomed bungalow in affluent Giffnock.

Ben and Annie had one son, Barney, but their family was extended because they adopted a boy called Sydney from Kinder transported children, brought up Ruth who was Annie's sister daughter, whose mother had died just six days after giving birth to her and Annie's sister, Esme, who had moved to Glasgow from Leeds. Ben coped with married life by staying away from it mostly. Annie was a difficult woman and Barney, from a young age, was beginning to display some of the behavioural issues inherited from his mother. Ben's way of dealing with this was to pay people to keep Barney in the mainstream, instead of dealing with the real issues.

There were real issues to be dealt with domestically mainly due to Annie's temperament. There were rumours within the Jewish community that Ben was involved in a long-term affair with Esme, who was the exact opposite of her sister. She was kind and gentle and well liked, whereas Annie was avoidable. It was noted that when he bought his wife an expensive fur coat, he also bought one for Esme – this was definitely not a buy one, get one free offer. Barney continued to develop mental health issues and was not in any way sociable like his father. Ruth trained as a ballet dancer, then ran away from home to live with her husband's family who were travelling showmen, and Sydney went on to be a professional poker player. Ben, either by choice or involuntarily, just carried on with his businesses and making money. He employed his son in his shop when he left school – a big mistake.

As I was saying earlier, Ben was tremendously successful, wealthy and lucky. When the government legalised bookmaking, he became a Tote bookie. The tool shop was thriving due to the economic boom in construction in Glasgow during the 1960s and his continued service. To give you an idea of just how wealthy he was and how lucky he was, I will tell you this story.

One day, Ben hired a plane to take him and some other bookies and friends down to Goodwood racing in Sussex from

Glasgow. Ben and his bookmaking friends took their satchels to work and make money at this prestigious race meeting, others just went for a fun-filled few days. Can you imagine how much that would have cost him to do that just a few years after rationing was still existent in Britain. He was loaded. The next part of the story was that after making a fortune at the races, the plane crashed near Largs during a violent thunderstorm. No one should have survived, however, the blessed Ben and his co-travellers walked away unscathed in their stocking soles, as the blast had blown their shoes off. The newspapers called it a miracle. He carried on regardless but he was shaken.

Ben's demise came suddenly when he died of a heart attack, aged only 64. Many blamed it on the stress and strain brought on from the demands of his family or the trauma of the plane crash, but we'll never know why he was taken. What we do know is that Ben's legacy and good fortune did not last for any future generations. He left his wife a comfortable fortune that she was able to live on for the rest of her life, but his business did not survive. He left his son to run the shop, but Barney was ill equipped to do so. He did not possess the skills and personality to do so. Barney ended up as a semi-professional musician, but due to his temperament and lack of social skills, he chased away loyal customers. He squandered what was left of his dad's fortune.

If only Ben had not swept the problems within his family under the carpet, things could and should have been so much better.

Broken – It Is Now

Martin's appointment card arrived from Canniesburn Hospital and confirmed his admission for Monday, 12th July, 1976, and his operation two days later. The surgery was the culmination of years of work to minimise the effect of a cleft palate. The final objective was to enhance Martin's appearance and create a socially acceptable persona. The doctors told him it would be life changing, and so it proved.

He was just 21, employed in the National Savings Bank in Glasgow, had successfully completed school, emerging with decent qualifications, lived within a close and loving family environment, had countless friends and oozed confidence and charisma. The decision to undergo this operation was major. Martin was reluctant, feeling he already possessed all of the above. His parents did not pressurise him, but he eventually decided to take the surgeon's advice and talked himself into believing he needed it.

The operation involved inserting bone into his cheeks from his hips, to enhance his facial structure and to bring his top teeth in front of his bottom set. This was to be achieved by breaking his jaws, and setting the bones which were to be held together through metal pins drilled into his skull and chin. Right, Martin really needed that done to him.

He kept his appointment, hesitantly. He was being hypothetically analytical. He was thinking, *What am I giving up? Socially, it's the time of my life. This is the finest summer in years and my charismatic powers are endless. Here I am, living like a celebrity guest, constantly being invited to weddings, engagements and parties. I don't really know why but I seem to be able to entice friendship naturally. You name it – I'm always invited. Maybe, I already have that socially acceptable persona*. The doubts about the need for these procedures stayed in his mind but as always, Martin always took the advice of professionals, older people who knew better than him.

Martin's time in the hospital was an adventure. He sort of thought that it was spooked when, on the first day he was in hospital, he was visited by his uncle, Bobby. Now, Bobby turned up rather worse for wear. Initially, he was complaining because the ward was too hot, then he started to loosen his collar, before Martin had to go and fetch him some water and finally, he had to lie him down on the bed while he searched for a nurse to give him medical attention and revive him as he had fainted. Martin could have been forgiven for wondering who was visiting whom.

Martin spent the first few days familiarising himself with his surroundings and his ward mates. He was placed in ward 7, a four-bedded suite. The other three beds were occupied by some diverse characters. Firstly, there was Jim, an octogenarian having surgery on a badly burned leg. He suffered from dementia as he blethered to himself all day. Just as well as no one ever came to visit him.

Secondly, there was Tommy from Mayhill in Glasgow. He was having a thumb, which had been lost in an industrial accident, grafted on through his chest, using bone from his hip and skin from his thigh. Tommy amused Martin greatly. He used to skip out most afternoons to enjoy romantic liaisons with his wife and visits to his local pub. He usually returned in high spirits. He would buzz the nurses to soothe his thigh, claiming he was in agony. His ploy worked every time. Martin, in his youthful naivety, asked him how he managed it with his thumb, only to be told that was not the part of his anatomy he was using.

The third guy was John. He was transgender and was about to have a sex change operation. He was from the south side of Glasgow. He and Martin recognised each other immediately, but did not speak to each other due to the sensitive nature of his operation and to avoid embarrassment. The silence didn't hold for long though after Martin's brother

Matt came to see him, and immediately saw John. He uttered these mortifying words,

"How's Aud, is this you in for your strapadictomy?"

Martin was mortified but the ice was broken, and he actually got to know John so well. He respected him for what he had gone through and was able to ask him all the questions you ever wanted to know, but were afraid to ask. Martin didn't know how John and his family survived and just couldn't imagine being trapped in the wrong body.

The next day, Martin's operation took place. He had no memories apart from coming too by Friday. He surmised by his mum's distress that he was no oil painting. His sister brought him a mirror. What a sight! Two big, black eyes, a metal scaffold screwed into his skull, gums entwined and a tiny gap for liquid food.

Temporarily, Martin continued his recuperation. He had really happy memories. He had tons of visitors, all-embracing all four patients. There was lots of banter and humour. His dad visited every day and emotionally blackmailed him about his efforts for the rest of his life. Martin recalled his friend, Robin, who missed his vocation as a stand-up comedian, using his visits as a platform to entertain them all with his jokes and endless funny tales. Martin seemed to be progressing and returned home after two and half weeks, although the metal frame had to stay on for a further five and a half weeks. He was fading away due to lack of food.

Once he was home, his mum cleaned up his hip wound. He kept the metal frame polished. Martin began to worry somewhat as puss was oozing from his hip. His dad called the doctor, who diagnosed an infection and prescribed antibiotics which helped to stem the flow. He was counting the days until the metal frame was removed and his gums were freed and he could eat solid food again. The stress began to take its toll on him. As you know, six weeks' confinement to a twenty-one-year-old is like a life sentence.

D-Day arrived. Martin went to the outpatients to have the scaffold dismantled and the metal brace detached. Disaster struck. He could feel the screwdriver loosening the structure from his head. It was literally a huge weight lifted. He felt lightheaded. The next stage of the process was to snap the wires holding the iron dentures surrounding his teeth. As soon as the oxygen reached his lungs, as his mouth was opened for the first time in eight weeks, he began to be violently sick.

He regained his composure for the last part which was to disengage the brace from his teeth. His world disintegrated-for when the doctor pulled the brace down, all his front teeth, bar one, fell out with the glue from the brace. He was shell-shocked. This was supposed to enhance his attractiveness and there he was looking like Albert Steptoe on a bad day. Apart from looking awful, Martin was also feeling awful. His worst fears were realised.

As the weeks passed, his physical condition deteriorated. He was constantly cold, tired and puss was still exuding from his hip, which now resembled an active volcanic crater. He was in so much pain. His dad could take no more and took him to the A&E in Glasgow.

When he got there, his hip was x-rayed. There was an ominous silence. He sensed something was wrong. The staff told him that he would have to be transferred to Canniesburn Hospital where the original operation had been performed. Martin and his dad were dispatched in an ambulance with a note. On reaching the hospital, Martin was told that a foreign body was causing his hip infection and that it would have to be removed via another operation. He was being poisoned to death. He was operated on and the offending gauze swab was removed. It was now late September and summer was gone.

The following few weeks were horrendous for Martin. He was examined by his work doctor and threatened with dismissal. His whole social life had collapsed, pending his denture adventure. His confidence drained away. The rewards for all the suffering were meaningless as all the work, which had been carried out in the years before, had been ruined. It felt like the last piece in the jigsaw didn't fit. The only benefits Martin derived from this episode were the ability to put life into perspective and to find out who his real friends were. It took him years to recover from this ordeal at the hands of the professionals.

When he was strong enough to be philosophical and had moved on from the feelings of bitterness created by this cruel spell of bad luck, Martin consoled himself with the knowledge that he was privileged to enjoy a normal mainstream education, which would not have been possible were it not for the medical profession. He appreciated the motivation he had been given to sustain employment. He developed as a person, able to appreciate the problems that other people had to endure in their life and how human nature is always resolute in times of adversity. His favourite saying is 'If it's not broken, don't fix it'.

Calendar Girl

They first met 20 years ago at Eleanor's surprise 50th birthday party. They remembered being seated together with their partners, who since then had sadly passed on. They were now attending Eleanor's surprise 70th birthday party. They both recalled the first occasion so well, especially when they watched the video tape Eleanor's husband, Allan, had produced. Jack was 81 now and Jenny was 70. They were seated together again, in the singleton's corner. Jack complemented Jenny on how little she had changed in the intervening 20 years and she reciprocated.

As the evening wore on, they chatted about how they had adapted to life without their partners. Jenny had busied herself working within the Women's Institute. Jack had continued to work up to six years ago. He spent his time now joining groups and socialising with friends old and new. He had developed a penchant for singing karaoke and enjoyed dancing. They were both enjoying full lives. Jack, an incurable flirt, was keen to demonstrate his dancing skills and before too long, asked Jenny to dance. They were getting on really well. They were happy to reconnect because everyone seemed to be part of a couple and they were alone. During the evening, Jack seized the opportunity to sing one of his favourite songs, *Calendar Girl*, and then, *I Can't Help Falling in Love with You*. Jenny was impressed with his *joie de vivre* and general zest and attitude. She loved his sense of humour and warmed to his pleasant conversation. At the end of the evening, they parted company but exchanged telephone numbers and promised to keep in touch.

A few days later and much to Jack's amazement, Jenny called to say that she had two tickets for the Edinburgh Tattoo but no one to go with. Jack promptly accepted her offer. They arranged to meet at his house. She would have to stay overnight as she lived in Dumfriesshire, the show was in the capital and he lived in Glasgow. Jack started to panic as soon as he put the phone down. He was going to have to do some housework. He hadn't had any sleepovers since his wife died. What would the sleeping arrangements be? What to expect – he didn't know.

Was this the start of a romance? He had many opportunities and created many friendships with women since his wife died, but he had never really taken it any further than platonic friendship – he was too scared of his daughter's reaction.

On the day of the Tattoo, Jenny arrived at Jack's house. He took her to a local Italian restaurant before they set off for Edinburgh by train. They enjoyed the colourful show and headed back to his place. Jack invited Jenny to sleep in his bed and he slept in the smaller spare bedroom. They both felt comfortable about that arrangement. The next morning, Jack prepared breakfast and Jenny left for home in the afternoon. Again, the night had been a success. They enjoyed the show, each other's company and Jack said the next night out was on him as Jenny had paid for the Tattoo tickets.

The next day, he couldn't wait to tell all his friends in the walking group about his newfound friendship. Now this group of people were a shower of remorseless mickey-takers, who took it upon themselves to develop this liaison into a romance.

"Oh! When's the engagement?"

"Can I be a bridesmaid?"

"You know you can get Viagra over the counter at Boots!"

…as well as other acerbic remarks as to what a quick mover he was.

"You're too old to be a bridesmaid. If I do get engaged, can I get one of those rings you never returned? And for your information – I don't need any chemical enhancement," he defended himself stoutly against their jibes.

Jack couldn't get Jenny out of his mind. He wanted to meet her again. He went to King's Theatre and booked two tickets for *Grease the Musical*. He thought she would enjoy that. He called her that night; Jenny was more than pleased to accept his invitation to see the show and stay the night. Another success. Things were going really well.

As you can imagine, when he shared the news of this next date night, he was the talk of the steamie. He thought he had left a lot of disappointed ladies on the shelf as they derided his efforts.

"Tell me more, tell me more – did she put up a fight?"

"I suppose she'll be hopelessly devoted to you."

The walkers were enjoying the banter, but the affair took another twist.

A couple of days later, Jenny called again, "Jack, you're going to have to come down here. I've forgotten to give you your passport back after the Tattoo. Fancy staying a few days? Bring enough clothes for an extended break and we'll see how it goes."

Jack was again pleasantly surprised that she seemed as keen on a relationship as he was. The next night, he was visiting a friend as he had done every Tuesday night for the last 10 years.

"By the way, Willie, I won't be able to come up next Tuesday – going down to Dumfriesshire to stay with Jenny for a few days. She mistakenly kept hold of my passport after the Tattoo, and I need to get it back."

"Whoa!" said Willie, taken aback, "Steady on, tiger. Jack, this sounds to me like a potential honey trap. Keeping your passport – A hostage situation if I ever heard one."

"I hope so!" chortled Jack.

"Jack, you cannae trust these Women's Institute ladies. It's not all crocheting and flower arrangements, you know. Did you not read about those women who stripped off and made a calendar? For all you know, she could be a Miss Naughty November or Amorous April," Willie added.

"You're making her sound more attractive by the minute," he chuckled.

"You just watch yourself but I'll phone, just to make sure you're OK and you're not chained to some bedpost or a radiator. Remember many a word said in jest," Willie grinned. "My God, I don't believe it they used to call her the Olympic Torch, cos she never went out."

"You're just jealous, Willie. Don't phone for at least three days. If she is intending to restrain me, I'll give her three days to stop it. By the way, you've got some imagination. It is all just completely platonic and innocent," Jack retorted.

"We'll see, you know your problem, you've got the right to silence but you just don't have the ability, do you?"

Part Two?

The next week, Willie was sitting at home watching television with his wife when the telephone rang. It was Jack's daughter, Julie.

"Willie, is my dad up at yours tonight? I have been phoning him all day, but there's no answer and I am beginning to get worried."

Willie don't want to reveal her dad's whereabouts in case it wasn't what Jack would have wanted,

"Don't worry, Julie, he is probably tied up at the moment, or he lost his mobile again. I'm sure he'll call in. I let you know if I hear from him and tell him to contact you – OK?"

After she hung up, Willie thought he had better phone him to ask him to contact his daughter as she did sound concerned. The old bugger should have told her where he was anyway.

"Hi, Jack, where are you? I just had Julie on the phone, frantic with worry as you were not returning her calls. What should I tell her or will you phone her?"

"Willie, I am having a great time in Puerto Del Carmen with Jenny. Turns out, she used my passport to book a holiday. I've lost my innocence but I found a friend. I even found a karaoke bar!" he sounded pleased with himself.

"Did you sing *Calendar Girl* to her? Phone Julie and I'll catch up when you get home. If you can't be good, be careful."

A Cat's Tale

It was a bright, misty spring morning in Pollokshields. The sun was just warm enough to evaporate the frost which had formed on the roof tiles after a freezing cold night. Kulwant looked out of the window as she busied herself cleaning the house. She decided she would open her windows. It was the first time she had felt like doing that in months. The house was very warm as she had given up on trying to economise on her heating costs, since her mother had come to live with them. Her mum was a pensioner and so, they had joined the Saveheat Plan, meaning they could use as much gas and electricity as they wanted because the bill was price capped. Kulwant felt this was a blessing as she was so cold-livered, almost anaemic. Mizbah, the family cat, was following her around the house as she hoovered and dusted her way through the upstairs of the house.

Oh! Thank Christ, em…I mean Allah, thought Mizbah, as she leapt from the carpet onto the windowsill, *fresh air!*

Mizbah had been housebound since she first came to the family as a Christmas present for the two boys, Sanji and Surf. She had been apprehensive when she came here at first, as she had heard a lot of rumours about what foreigners do to cats. She found these rumours to be completely unfounded; she had never been better looked after. She had only ever seen the outside of the house from a cage. It had been dark and cold when she was brought to her new home. It was a fantastic, big house, but she had covered every inch of it and even, though she was a cat, she found the heat in the house overwhelming. At first, the heat was welcoming, but she needed respite and sitting on the window ledge was so cool – she could see it all there.

Mizbah was thinking to herself, *Gawd, here ur moanin'
aboot the swelter. Jist imagine what it wis like a few months
ago. There ah wis up in Easterhoose, stuck wi' a cupple a
brass monkeys. I hid to be rescued by the Cat Protection
League efter they bastards left the hoose empty wi' me in it –
sleepin'. The hoose got boardit up wi' me inside it! Did ah
yam and yam? Ma life was saved by auld Nellie fae up the
sterr complainin'. Ma name was Molly then, I wis a Prodalic.
Noo, hark at me – too hoat – that's a laff, innit?*

The ginger cat continued to perch on the window ledge.
Mizbah was surveying the scene around her. She had a bird's
eye view of the whole neighbourhood. It was lovely, full of
detached townhouses. The area was predominately Asian.
Some people referred to the estate as Banglashields because
most of the inhabitants were from Asia. Asia was all around.
Halal butchers, fruit and veg shops, newsagents and the
omnipresent smell of curry and the scurry of white vans.

Mizbah spotted a bird's nest, snuggled up against a
drainpipe. She could see there were five squawking chicks
waiting to be fed by their absent parents. She started to assess
the logistics. She was quite high up. The sill was slippery. The
melting rime made it risky. Her instincts were telling her to
go for it, just to prove that she still could. On the other hand,
the nest was slightly out of reach and this made it a precarious
venture. Mizbah wasn't really that hungry, she always had
plenty of food readily available – but still. She was undecided
– could it wait for better conditions? Maybe aye, maybe no?

Mizbah's attention was distracted. There was a lot going
on in the street that morning. The next-door neighbour, who
she had never yet met, appeared to be moving out. A big,
maroon furniture removal van had arrived with the belongings
of the new residents. The curiosity got the better of her as she
lost focus on the prospective snack, and began to concentrate
on the contents of the van. Any sign of children? Toys? What
about pets – maybe company, maybe a rival? Her mind was
working overtime. Her concentration was affected by the
whirring of the hoover in the next room.

Mizbah once again turned her attention to the nest. She had spotted the mother returning earlier. She was thinking about it again when her concentration was disturbed. Sanji and Surf had arrived home from school for their lunch. Kulwant was so busy running after her mother and tidying up, she hadn't prepared anything for them. The boys had been sent up to their room to watch television until their lunch was ready. They started off playing in their own room, but eventually ended up in their mum's bedroom where Mizbah was. They were making a helluva racket and putting Mizbah off.

The ginger cat was getting annoyed. She had looked at all the angles and tried to judge the best way she could reach the defenceless chicks without knocking over the pot plants, or even worse, slipping from the ledge. She focused, she stealthily hid her frame behind the pot and stretched out an extended paw. She missed. She had to rethink her strategy, she was getting cold, and feeling hungry and pride was beginning to become an issue.

Nothing was going to stand in her way. She was determined she was having an alfresco lunch. She maneuvered herself nearer to the edge of the sill. Totally focused, oblivious to the noise of the traffic or the racket coming from the house. She, once again, reached out a paw,

Gotcha!

Then, *WHAM!* The next thing she knew, a ball came flying through the air from inside the house. Surf screamed as he realised that he had unbalanced Mizbah, and knocked her off the window ledge. Mizbah was gobsmacked. She immediately let go of the terrified chick as she headed for the ground at great speed.

Mercifully, Allah was good. Mizbah hurtled through the air and landed slap bang in the middle of the trampoline which hadn't been taken down. She was one lucky moggie. All of the family rushed towards the garden. Mizbah was stunned. She wasn't hurt, but her pride had taken a blow. She hoped no one had seen this unfortunate incident. She didn't want her reputation to be in tatters before she had even built it. She was carried once again into the warmth of the house and pampered and fed and watered. What a life!

Mizbah was just thinking to herself as she soaked up the heat, *You can take the cat oot fae Easterhoose, but you cannae take Easterhoose oot the cat. Be sure, that wee bugger is gonnae find a nasty surprise under his bed afore this day is oot.*

Christmas in Paradise

Charlie was overwhelmed when the man from P&O phoned to tell him that he had won a trip on a luxury cruise liner sailing around the Oceanic Islands, leaving on December 23rd and returning on 7th January. It was great news because he had never been to that part of the world. He was going to be 80 on Christmas Day, and this would have been his first Christmas spent alone as his wife had sadly passed away just six months before. His family were not too happy for him and wanted him to postpone his trip as they had planned a special festive program for him, but Charlie wouldn't have it. It was a once in a lifetime opportunity and he wasn't going to miss out. He could have taken someone with him, but he didn't want to ask friends to be away from family at Christmas, nor did he want to ask anyone from his OAP club because they all made him feel old. Charlie just took the cash equivalent as a prize.

Charlie checked the itinerary. He couldn't believe his luck. He was being flown from London to Sydney, then onto the cruise liner, to places he had only associated with pointless answers before. He was going to Tonga, Tuvalu, Marshall Islands and Vanuatu, then finishing off back in Sydney and being brought back home first class. Charlie had never been on a cruise before so he asked all the folks he knew that what attire he needed, what money he would require and what to expect when he was on-board.

The trip out was everything Charlie expected and more. Luxury all the way, champagne breakfasts on the plane, his every need catered for. It was a long flight, but it was so much easier doing it in style. Etihad Airlines provided the best food, the most comfortable seats and the customer service on-board just blew Charlie away. The flight was effortless for him. He arrived in Sydney jet-lagged and weary but happy. He wondered what it would have been like if he was not given the luxury treatment. He was driven from the airport to his hotel. He was to spend 24 hours there to give him time to recover from the flight. Then, the exciting bit – the cruise.

He arrived on-board on Christmas Eve. He was given a guided tour of the important logistics on the ship and allocated to his opulent cabin. He had never seen such sumptuous luxury. Gold-plated china, gold-plated phone, en suite bathroom, four-poster bed with the silkiest linen and on-board service at the push of a button 24/7. Charlie thought he had died and gone to heaven. He checked out the ship's brochure to see what facilities were available. Umpteen different types of restaurant service, swimming pools, saunas, gym, ballrooms, casinos, libraries and bars. He unpacked his clothes and prepared for the start of the cruise.

The boat left Sydney Harbour at 8:00 local time. It was still warm and sunny. There were hundreds of people waving their loved-ones off. Charlie hadn't even thought of home once. He took in the sights. Charlie saw sights he thought he never would. The Opera House, the Harbour Bridge, Bondi Beach, the Rocks, as the ship maneuvered through Port Jackson. The next day was Christmas. He was looking forward to the ball at Captain's Table. This was going to be Charlie's first ever black-tie do – he was excited.

The ship smoothed and slithered through the water to its next destination. Charlie mainly spent the day taking photographs from the top deck and eating. He had never seen so much good quality food in all his life. He thought, *If this is how the other half live – I want to live like this*. When it was time, he retired to his chalet to ready himself for the ball. He imagined that he may feel a little strange as he was there on his own and most people were with their partners. Nothing could have been further from the truth. There were plenty of WAGS, but a fair percentage were passengers travelling on their own. Charlie was shocked when the captain made the announcement that not only was it a special day because it was Christmas, but that a member of the audience was celebrating a special birthday. Charlie was summoned to the top table and presented with a magnum of champagne – Dom Pérignon – no less. Charlie thought this trip was getting better and better.

The atmosphere at the ball was fantastic as the Michael Buble tribute act got the night started. The crowd were raring to go by the time Tony Christie came on. The ball was formal but also relaxed. Charlie, then, was given the shock of his life. A middle-aged lady approached him and asked him if he would dance with her. Charlie was flattered indeed. Charlie thought there was a striking resemblance between her and his daughter, Jane. Same bone structure, colouring and same-shaped eyes. The woman was asking Charlie a lot of questions about himself as if seeking confirmation. After their dance, Alicia asked Charlie if he would like to meet her mother. She told him that it may be a surprise for him. It wasn't a surprise, it was a staggering, earthmoving shock. He had just been introduced to Margaret, his very first girlfriend. He had not seen her for 63 years since she immigrated with her parents to Australia. They were both left heartbroken, but had gone on to marry other partners. They were both recently widowed. This was kismet.

Charlie and Margaret and Alicia were inseparable for the rest of the evening. Charlie couldn't believe what was happening to him. They chatted about times gone by and arranged to meet the next day and the days after. They travelled together through Oceania, sightseeing all the ports and islands in the area. They dined together, they wined together, they danced together and they had so much fun reminiscing. Margaret's daughter encouraged her mother's flirting. She kept herself busy sunbathing and getting pampered on the ship. The days passed too quickly for Charlie. Soon, it was the final day of the cruise. Charlie had fallen for Margaret all over again and she for him. Charlie went to bed. He thought of the last time he had slept with Margaret, the day before her parents separated them by continent. He woke alone. He lay there pondering whether or not to remain in Australia or go back home. He could not help himself from imagining who Alicia's dad might be. After giving it minimal thought, he decided to remain in the Southern Hemisphere and take on whatever developed. He was going to tell Margaret the next day.

Charlie was awoken with a sound coming through the tannoy:

"This is your captain speaking, please remain in your cabins until otherwise informed. We would ask you not to worry. The doors on the cabin have been automatically locked for your own protection. I will inform you of further developments," he said calmly.

Charlie looked out of his window down onto the harbour side. He could see the port was crawling with police vehicles and dogs. He wondered what was wrong. Surely not terrorists? Or a robbery? The next sight he saw was Margaret and Alicia being escorted off the liner in handcuffs. She glanced up at him looking out of his chalet window. She was crying as she was led away with her daughter. The temporary inconvenience caused by this bizarre incident was quickly over and normal service was resumed. The doors were unlocked as the captain announced:

"Thank you all for your patience and perseverance during this time. You may now leave your cabins and resume your daily plans. All the restaurants are now open and will be delighted to serve you the breakfast of your choice. Please enjoy the rest of your day on-board before you disembark. I know many of you have long journeys ahead. I hope this event has not spoilt your enjoyment of this wonderful cruise. On behalf of myself and the other crew members I wish you all bon voyage!"

Charlie was bemused. He found out unofficially that Margaret and Alicia had been hoodwinking vulnerable pensioners on cruise ships for a long time. They had swindled people out of hundreds and thousands of pounds by befriending solo travellers, stealing gold credit cards, finding out personal PIN numbers and emptying bank accounts. They never bankrupted anyone, just took a few thousand dollars which they hoped would not be noticed by their wealthy victims, however, they had been monitored over several cruises and, although this was the only cruise where no criminal activity had taken place, the police decided they had enough evidence to charge them. The only thing that Charlie found missing were a pair of Stewart tartan underpants, which he thought he had placed under his pillow the night before. Hardly a crime of the century. Charlie never saw Margaret again as she was subsequently jailed for six years and died in prison. Charlie went home to Scotland having had the time of his life, wondering if he had just had a great escape.

Downtown

It's really strange, but the town looks and is different at different times of the day and depends how you are getting around. If you are riding on the bus, and you get a window seat, and there is no condensation, you can observe the hustle and bustle of the pedestrians in Shawlands, witness the frustrations of the drivers at the roundabouts, watch the people in the park at the pond feeding the ducks and swans – all that before you even get into the heart of the city. You can admire the people travelling by train for they are going faster than you and they are higher, so they can see more than you. You observe the cyclist getting in the way, the walkers marching into offices and when you get off the bus, the homeless people, who have spent the night sleeping under the Hielanman's Umbrella, using their Greggs coffee cups to beg for handouts, while the workers make their way into the call centres and shopping malls. The cleaners are all going back out of town, the streetcleaners are starting their shift, making sure the city centre is spruced up. They go up Buchie, down Sauchie and along the Gyle. The tourist buses have already started – very early in the summer. I decided this was probably the best way to see the sites, and there is plenty to see. Museums, bridges, galleries and parks, that's Glasgow from the morning perspective.

Travelling by train during the day is different. On the East Kilbride line, there are many fine panoramic views. You are looking down onto the road traffic-jams everywhere. The trains are usually silent, people reading kindles, sending texts, checking laptops, reading papers or just staring out the windows. There are loads of bowling clubs en route. You can watch the pensioners, all dressed in white, following the necessary etiquette, before retiring into the wooden clubhouses for a bite to eat or a drink. The congestion thickens nearer the centre, making you feel glad that you chose the train. The train arrives at busy Central Station. People staring up at the timetable board to find out which platform to move to. Some have been shopping, some going to work and college. Groups of people hang about the station. Emo's, punks and pensioners everywhere.

Emerging from the stations, the city is alive. Pedestrian precincts full. Buskers at every corner, Roma buskers strumming local tunes only known to them, Marc Bolan tribute singers and sales in all the designer shops, trying to attract customers with luminous large signs. The bars and restaurants have introduced a relatively new phenomenon; eating and drinking outside. I don't get it, but it is very popular and continental. Unfortunately, the weather isn't.

People come into the light from the underground, the entrances of these buildings also seem to attract singers of all qualities. The poshest one is in Buchanan St. A sea of people is the best way to describe the consumers using this thoroughfare. Designer stores, John Lewis at the top, House of Fraser at the bottom, the rest in between, what more could you ask for, and live music everywhere. People from all different parts of the world can be seen. It's not as big as London or New York, but it is just as cosmopolitan.

Night time is different again, specially Friday nights. Lots of partygoers who went out straight from work. The city lights highlight the silver-domed concert halls which have replaced theatres. The Hydro and SECC are big multifunctioning arenas with no atmosphere to speak of. You can see Parkhead Stadium lights, but the real action is in the Merchant City – the style mile. Restaurants and bars vying for customers. All nationalities of food and tastes catered for. The people leaving their work do's early, bump into the people just starting their night out late. Young, scantily clad girls in high heels, stumbling towards clubs, older drunk men trying to find their way to taxi ranks, bouncers checking that clients are over 21 and the sound of music pervading the carnival atmosphere. I love Glasgow.

Ella – A Real Life Story

Ella was a happy, carefree girl who lived in the Perthshire countryside. Her days were spent rambling in the neighbouring fields and, at harvest time, picking fruit for the local farmer, who paid the children in punnets. Everything in her life was idyllic until tragedy struck. The poor soul's mother died in a winter flu-epidemic which suddenly hit Central Scotland. Ella was only nine at the time of her mother's demise. She felt vulnerable, but mainly sad. She was the youngest of three, but her brother and sisters both lived in other parts of the world and had their own children to raise, so they could not be too involved in bringing her up. In all honesty, her dad felt he was more than capable of carrying out this task himself.

It was just after the war, 1948 in fact, two years after her mother passed away, her father, who was the stationmaster, married his second wife. She was a spinster who had no time for children, particularly one like Ella who needed a lot of love, affection and attention. Ella's life simmered on. The relationship between Ella, who was now an insecure teenager, and her stepmother deteriorated daily. If it was hate at first sight, this negativity festered into cruelty and bitchiness and downright spite. Her father seemed oblivious. Ella did not tell him half the tricks her stepmother had gotten up to. She knew he would never believe how this crone had forced her into a life of servitude.

There were few good moments in her life, but things took a turn for the worse when suddenly Ella's father was struck down by a massive heart attack and died immediately. Ella was nearly 15 now. She was about to leave school and had planned to get a job and save as hard as she could to rent a place of her own in Perth. However, her stepmother had other ideas.

It was a cold Saturday morning, Ruth, the stepmother, had packed Ella's clothes and informed her that since she needed time to get over her husband's death, she was sending her down to relatives in Pollok, Glasgow for a few days. Ella and Ruth took the train down to smoky Queen Street station. There they were met by Ella's uncle, Sam, aunt, Sally and cousin, Harry. Ruth handed over some letters to Ella's aunt and embarked on the train back to Perth. She never even glanced back.

Ella and her relatives, who were largely unknown to her, took the train to the outskirts of the south side of Glasgow. Ella was amazed to see row upon row of slums, tenements and houses spread throughout the city. She was a country girl who was used to village life. Ella was frightened and alone but she was still glad to be away from Ruth.

They arrived back at her aunt's house in Pollok. It was situated in a housing scheme, but not in a close. Aunt Sally's house was a four-in-block cottage flat. They all sat down, and Sally went to make a cup of tea. She showed Ella the room she would be sleeping in, and the other rooms in the house.

"Ella," she said in a hushed voice, "there's no way of dressing up what I am about to say to you."

The two men got up and left the room. They knew what bombshell was coming and did not fancy the reaction.

"Ella, you are to stay here permanently. Your stepmother doesn't want you and is refusing to keep you in Perth. She has sent you down here and I am now your legal guardian."

Ella was shocked speechless. She burst into tears. It was nothing personal against her aunt and uncle, as she hardly knew who they were. It was just the impact of moving from one culture to another without any warning. She did not know Glasgow or anyone in it. At 15, she just had to do what she was told.

Her aunt comforted her. She told her not to worry, she would be all right with her. She took Ella into her new bedroom and told her she would see her in the morning. The

52

next day, Ella was exhausted. She barely slept all night as she familiarised herself with her lodgings. Her aunt prepared breakfast and told her what she had planned for her.

"One of my friends has a hairdressing shop in Shawlands, she has offered to take you on as an apprentice. I have accepted her offer on your behalf, and I've booked you a place at Cardonald College where you will complete your training course. I will expect you to pay your way. Dig money will be five shillings per week. That leaves you with five shillings. I expect you to save from this. I expect you to keep yourself and your room clean and tidy. Lights go out in this house at 9:30 pm. You can start work at 9:00 am tomorrow. I will make your pieces. Any questions?"

There were none. Ella did as she was told. She followed Sally's instruction and travelled on the number 23 tram down to Shawlands. She got off the tram and walked into the salon 'Manes by Maud'. Ella was greeted warmly by her new employer who knew all about her family history from Sally. She empathised with her as she herself had been orphaned at a very young age. Ella settled quickly into work. She had never given a thought to a career in hairdressing, but thought she would give it a go as her aunt had been kind enough to arrange it for her. The shop was quiet, so Maudy had plenty of time to show her the ropes and coach her to a high standard. She went to college once a week, and this helped her to meet new people and integrate with Glaswegians. Ella was a solitary, shy girl who did not mix too well, but she had been thrown in at the deep end and had to befriend her fellow students, hard-arsed and worldly-wise as they were, if she was to make a life in Glasgow.

As far as working was concerned, things were going swimmingly well and Ella discovered she had a natural flair for dressing hair, however, on the home front, it was a different story.

Sally and Sam were all right. They treated her fairly and looked after her. They were strict, but that was what life was like and older people had authority and commanded respect from younger people. Ella would not have dreamt of crossing them, especially as she had nowhere else to go. The problem was their son, Harry. At first, he was very polite to Ella, but as the weeks progressed, his behaviour changed as it became obvious that the attraction was not mutual. He started by brushing against her at every opportunity, and then he would pinch her bottom as she passed by when his parents weren't watching. Ella resisted his charms and made it plain she was not interested in him. She avoided being alone with him whenever she could. He would try to force himself upon her. She always resisted, but as time moved on, she was feeling more and more uncomfortable in her aunt's house. She realised she was going to have to move out before a serious incident occurred. Harry was getting heavy with her and was not happy at her refusal to co-operate with him. Her aunt and uncle had shown nothing but kindness to her, so, she did not want to upset them or offend them by telling on their son.

Ella, however, was soon to get her wish to leave her lodgings. She had been persuaded by a few college girls to go to a dance at the Plaza ballroom, a top nightspot in Glasgow. She had saved up to buy a beautiful, taffeta ball gown. It was her first night out on her own. Ella did not drink alcohol (it was not allowed in the house) but all her friends did. As the evening wore on, she became more isolated as most of the girls had paired off. Ella did not mind not being paired off. She was only 18 and hadn't been romantically involved before. She was just enjoying the atmosphere, learning how to refuse drunken men a dance and listening to the music being played by the live orchestra. She was sitting down when the bandleader announced the last waltz. Suddenly, and much to her surprise, one of the musicians left the stage and asked her to dance. She was excited. He was an older man, maybe 30-ish, but he was dapper and mature and well spoken.

Stanley Schlossoff wasn't a particularly good-looking chap. He was balding, rotund and experienced. Ella thought she had hit the jackpot when he asked her out to dinner the next night. She was impressed. He had given her a lift home in his brand-new Merc, she had ascertained that he had his own business, lived in an exclusive, leafy suburb, was a semi-professional musician and had all the trappings of wealth. He even made a silly excuse just to talk to her. Prince Charming had arrived – not!

Ella and Stan were married within three months of meeting. Ella had succumbed to her experienced suitor and he agreed to marry her. Ella had two children within 18 months of marriage. Soon after the wedding, it had all turned sour. It was a case of marry in haste, repent at leisure. Stan's business went bust, he was bankrupt, being sued by several clients and developing mental health issues, which made him abusive and aggressive. Ella was trapped in a loveless, poverty-ridden, depressing marriage. Stan's rages worsened and eventually had the effect of causing Ella to have a nervous breakdown. Ella was a broken woman but she still had to sustain her family. She did this by cutting hair in the backroom of their house. There was no other income available as Stan's behaviour rendered him unemployable. Her only saving grace was her weekly choir meetings. She had earlier converted to Judaism and to enhance her family's chances of acceptance into the community, joined the choir. Ella had a beautiful singing voice. Every week, her next-door neighbour, Nathan, also a Jewish man, would give her a lift to and from the choral meeting at the local synagogue. Nathan was in a dire marriage himself, so, he knew what she was going through. He could also hear Stan's rants through the wall. She had tried to persuade Stan to accept that he had mental health problems, but he wouldn't. Then, Ella, in a moment of weakness, had allowed herself to get pregnant again after a 12-year gap. She was at the end of her tether. Stan's depression and rages got even worse. She had another baby girl, but she had to be looked after by her teenage daughter. She had slipped, if not catapulted, into post-natal depression. Eventually, through counselling and drugs – she recovered. She knew she had to leave Stan for all of their sakes. She gave him one final chance to get help. He did not accept this opportunity, so she left him and moved into a rented flat in nearby Shawlands with her beleaguered children. She continued to work from home and saved up enough money to put down a deposit on her own shop in Shawlands.

Things were beginning to look up. Her older children had left school. One moved to London, the other married young. Ella was a single parent with an eight-year-old girl.

One night, she was sitting at home on her own when she heard a knock on the door. She opened the door and who was standing there, with a suitcase in his hand, but her old friend and neighbour, Nathan.

"Ella," he said sheepishly, "Can I come in? I've finally plucked up the courage to leave her. Couldn't stand it anymore."

"Nathan, come in, but you know my situation here. You can't stay. I've no room and people will talk."

However, Nathan and Ella did continue to see each other. At first, she was just helping him to get back on his feet, but eventually, after a long, cold feet period, love and romance blossomed. She had finally met her Prince Charming. She had a man who could offer her stability, security and love – all the things that had been taken from her. They both progressed to become successful business people and went on to celebrate their 35th wedding anniversary, which also happened by coincidence to be their 80th birthdays. In his tribute speech to her, he said he knew he had to be with her as soon as he heard her lovely singing voice. Although it had taken a long time for them to get together, each day they have is treasured.

Fat Chance

Fiona was a lovely child who always happy and smiling. She was very bright and sailed through school and university with ease. She had a textbook academic career, plenty of friends and a good love-filled family life. As a child, she could have been described as delightfully plump in the days when it was thought that if you were carrying a little extra weight it would be beneficial to you in case you had an illness, which meant you couldn't eat for a few days. The only issue she had was that as she grew into adolescence, it was becoming obvious that she was becoming noticeably overweight. She was still very attractive and had no problems in finding boyfriends etc., however, she was also starting to attract some rudeness connected to her size. She was able, at first, to rise above the remarks she overheard and continue confidently in her personal life and professional career. She was big and proud. She could often be seen in her skin-tight leopard skin trousers, a la Rod Stewart fashion, traipsing through town without a care in the world.

She married at quite a young age and, for the first time, her weight was beginning to cause her a problem. Her doctor advised her that she would increase her chances of conception if she lost some weight. She struggled and tried many diets unsuccessfully. The heavier she became, the more she craved food. Her fertility problems led her to comfort eating and the more she ate, the bigger she became. Her professional life was going well but, alas, her marriage ended through the strain of the physical and emotional limitations she was unable to control. She was spiralling into serious depression and was becoming obsessed with her weight, imagining that people were looking at her everywhere she went. She would go into business meetings and look to see if there was anyone as big as her, she began to hate using public transport as people clearly avoided sitting next to her, and she started to avoid eating in restaurants in front of other people. She realised she had to do something about it, but couldn't or wouldn't confront the issue head on. She wrote these words to console herself.

FATISM

Isn't it a little over the score?
When you don't want to go into work anymore?
Because your colleagues gloat and call you fat,
And implore you not to eat any of this, or that.

Why don't you become like me or him?
Why don't you be like us and join a gym?
Don't you know you're only five-foot-four?
Don't you know you should be ten stone, not an ounce more?

How about a lunchtime 10k run?
I tell you, this is such a lot of fun,
I bet you've never seen biceps such as these?
Not with you being morbidly obese.

In response, I'll tell you this,
Make no mistake, my shape is bliss,
I'd rather be cuddly and happy than be so vain,
People like you are such a pain.

It shouldn't matter how you look,
Bosses who harass should be brought to book,
Discrimination is too complex,
As is discussing your body mass index,

The size you are, doesn't matter,
Even if it does create some office patter,
But for those victims just like me,

You have my deepest sympathy.

Every day, I hope and dream,
They'll stop eating away at my self-esteem,
That they, just for once, leave me to brood,
People shouldn't be so downright rude.

The final straw came one day as she got off the train in Queen St Station, and could not walk up the hill on West Nile St to get to the top end of town. She had to stop every few yards. Then, to add insult to injury, there was a group of teenagers who had noticed her struggles, they started to fat shame her, hurling abuse at her, instead of trying to help her. She felt ashamed, hurt, embarrassed and angry and frustrated, as she hailed a taxi to take her 300 yards to her office. She decided enough was enough. She contacted her doctor and asked to be referred to Weight Management Services. She was now 23 stone and as low as she had ever been. On the night of that incident, she just couldn't delete those childish jibes from her head. Over and over again. She could not bear to hear those cruel words ever again.

She went along to the weight management meetings, expecting really just to gain some advice on how to lose weight. She had already tried multiple diet clubs and self-help, but nothing had ever worked. The first session was in a group. She was, at first, mortified as there was a delay in the doctor arriving at the meeting – the embarrassing silence. It was then that she realised what an epidemic she was a part of. The ice was broken when the doctor said:

"I'm sorry for your wait."

The group groaned in unison,

"We're sorry for our weight," the group joked.

The group sessions clearly displayed common themes all the participants were experiencing. Low self-esteem, mental health issues, but most of all, physical lives and relationships impeded by their behaviours and attitudes to food. After the group session, Fiona was then sent to a consultant who prescribed various different remedies to support her in losing weight. For the first time, she started to acknowledge the problems she was causing for herself. She started to respond to the advice she was given, and began to slowly lose weight. After the consultant was convinced about her commitment to improving her health, she was offered surgery in the form of a gastric sleeve. This surgery meant that she would lose 70% of her stomach, and her food intake and lifestyle would have to change dramatically forever. The doctor explained all the pre and post-operative requirements to her in graphic detail. She decided to go for it. She had her fill of discrimination, discomfort and distress. She was still 22 stone despite all her efforts, mainly due to her slow metabolic rate caused by inactivity.

The operation took place ironically on Mardi Gras. The surgeon made his incisions carefully, watching the screen displaying what he was doing. He saw the layers of mustardy-yellow fat, as thick clouds, that he had to grind his way through as though he was guiding an aeroplane to an airport. It was hard work getting through the clouds, but after an hour or so, he could see the beautiful landscape that was her body. He could see the healthy rose kidneys, the deep-red liver, the pink pancreas, the stretched stomach tissue, which he was about to remove, the stringy appendix still intact, the pallid gall bladder and the organs above and below all looking fabulous under the huge life-limiting cloud hovering above them. He could see that she had a great constitution as all her bits looked like they were still in working order. He made the incision and stitched her stomach back, reducing its size as he promised.

The next few weeks were hellish, but effective. Fiona's self-discipline and the discipline imposed by the operation were evidently working. The clouds were dissipating and her weight loss continued in the ensuing months that followed. Yes, she could only eat small amounts of food really slowly, yes it's true that her social life was affected, but what she had gained in mobility, health, fitness and self-esteem, had made the sacrifice worthwhile. She lost a further eight stone in six months. The dark clouds had disappeared from her mind and the mustardy-yellow layers of cloud were departing quickly to reveal the beautiful outer landscape of her body. Her confidence level spiralled upwards, and she had absolutely no regrets about undergoing the drastic surgery. She also finally managed that 10k run she wrote about.

Getting Over It

Chrissie was getting over it. It had been six months since John ran off with the next-door man's Thai bride and, even worse, emptied their joint bank account and point blank refused to pay for his daughter's upkeep. Chrissie told herself that if his conscious did not catch up with him, the law would. She was doing what had become her normal Saturday routine. She met her mum for shopping, then lunch, then a few drinks and then a few more drinks before going home. When she arrived home, the house was quiet. She did her usual and ordered a Chinese meal for herself and her daughter. She opened a bottle of Chardonnay from the fridge.

Half an hour later, the food arrived. She was expecting her daughter, Lisa, to arrive home any minute when her mobile went.

"Mum, just going to stop over at Kylie's tonight, is that OK?"

"OK, see you in the morning."

She felt herself getting slightly tipsier. She wondered what she was going to do with all that food. She thought for a minute and decided to knock on her next-door neighbour's door to see if he wanted to share it with her. She had not really had many conversations with him since his partner had sailed off into the sunset with her husband.

"Wan Hung Lo," she said, "do you like Chinese food?"

"Of course, I do. I from Hong Kong," he replied in his broken English /Chinese accent.

"Can I come in? I've got two Chinese meals to use up. Wanna share?"

"Hold on, wait a minute till I tidy up and then come."

He rushed into the living room to grab the remote control. He had been watching Thai porn as Chrissie just caught a glimpse of two cavorting bodies, before he was able to turn the television off. She thought this was quite amusing – catching him off guard. He gave her a gin and tonic and set the table for two. They engaged in small talk, carefully avoiding the big issue. He gave her some more gins whilst he drank mineral water. She was beginning to feel the effect of the booze. She felt relaxed and comfortable.

"So, how you really been, Wan Hung Lo?" Chrissie slurred.

"Very sad. Very ronery. I desperately need a rodger," he said, his eyes filling up.

Chrissie was taken aback by his forth righteousness, but quickly decided she would relieve him from his woes. She excused herself and went to the bathroom. The bathroom was beautiful. The walls were red and gold. There were ornate Chinese lanterns and scented candles everywhere. She was thinking revenge, after all Man-Ki had stolen her husband. Why shouldn't she have the last laugh, and take hers? She pondered for a few seconds and decided to go for it. Why not? She'd never been with anyone else before, it was time to really show she had moved on. She carefully removed and folded her clothes. She donned Man-Ki's fluffy, pink dressing gown, which was hung on the toilet door. She was feeling woozy. She stood against the warm radiator, with the thick towels hanging from it. She braced herself, took a big deep breath and sallied into the lounge. She sat on the couch and began to open up the dressing gown slowly.

"Well! Wang Hung Lo, what'd ya think?"

"Whoa! You madwoman! Why you come into my house and put on Man-Ki dressing gown? Why yo take you clothes off in my house? Get out, you madwoman!" he screamed in horror.

"But you said you were desperate!"

"Desperate to rent Man-Ki room to a rodger to help me pay mortgage!"

"Oh my God! Wan Hung Lo, I am so sorry, I completely misinterpreted what you said. Please delete this from your memory. I am mortified. I am just going to go."

Chrissie got dressed and made a hasty retreat next door. She was drunk. She went to her bed. She woke up early, the next morning. The events of the previous evening flashed back over her mind. She put the duvet over her head. She cringed with embarrassment. How could she ever look him in the eye again? How could she look at herself in the mirror? What if anyone else ever found out about it? Then, she thought well – what if? She had been prepared to move on and that was progress.

When she got up, she found a letter from Wan Hung Lo! It said, 'Thanks for the rubbery food.'. She knew what he meant.

Happy Meal

Will and Dorothy met up for the first time in a couple of years. It was a surprising venue as Dorothy requested to go to McDonalds. She was eighty and had never experienced the delight of a Big Mac. Will suggested that might be a bit too much for her, given her age and relative frailty. He was looking forward to meeting for this catch-up as he always found her really interesting, but had lost contact with her when she stopped coming to the art class through ill health. He had gone to great lengths to try to find her – just to know if she was getting better and if she needed his help. He bought her a bunch of flowers and gave her a huge, warm hug when they met in the car park. She was still driving. She was so pleased that he had taken the time out to look for her and to actually meet up with her. They had always been friendly but never bosom-buddies. She had often praised his drawings and encouraged him to develop his creative talents to the best of his ability. Will was never confident, so he really appreciated the feedback as it was genuine and, moreover, she had been an art teacher, so she knew what she was talking about. She was as unique and authentic a person as he had ever met. Although she was so much older than him, he felt a bond existed between them – kindred spirits. The kind of rapport you get when you meet someone for the first time, and you know instantly you are going to get along with them just fine, although there is no obvious link.

They found a quiet corner of the fast-food restaurant to sit. Will told her a cheeseburger or a Happy Meal were best suited to her appetite. She relented and explained that she didn't eat much these days. They exchanged pleasantries and Will went to the counter to order the food and drinks.

"Well!" he said in a concerned tone, "How have you been, Dorothy? Is your health good? I've been trying to find out for ages since you stopped using the class, but nobody seemed to know."

"Well!" she replied, "First of all, I have to tell you I am so blown away by your kindness. Do you know that people who I have known and associated with for years haven't even bothered to come and see me or even phone to see how am I am. Yet, you, a relative stranger go out of way, buy me flowers, take me for lunch and show me kindness. Thanks so much – you have no idea what that means to me. I am so disappointed with some people, but we live and we learn."

"No problem, Dorothy, the main thing is you seem well and strong and able, and that's good to see," said Will, "but are you as good as you look?"

"Son, where do you want to start? I can go from head to toe or toe to head – but what the hell, I'm still here and I'm going to make the most of whatever time I have left. I have lived a full life and I don't expect my best days are still to come, but I'm gonna keep trying! Believe you me."

"I don't doubt it for a minute. What have you been up to anyway?" he said.

"Well, I am still working. Don't know if you know, but I am a spiritualist and I do hypnotherapy. I actually meant to retire years ago, having successfully helped folk to contact their relatives, stop smoking and other addictions, but I keep on getting recommendations approaching me for help. It's awful – honestly, I thought if I overcharged them, it would make them go away but no matter how much I charge, they still come." She added, "Maybe, it's just as well because I usually use the money to bail out my kids – yes, even at their ages."

"My God, I didn't know you had that gift. When did you know you were able to see things?" Will enquired.

"Since I was a little girl when my parents brought me to this country. I could always see the world differently. I just did not understand what it was I had. For example, I can look at you and I see an orange aura around you," she said.

"What does that mean?" he quizzed.

"Don't worry. All good!" she said positively.

"When did you actually realise that you had special powers?" Will asked.

"It really came to the fore when I was at university in 1952. I just seemed to pick up things – particularly languages uncannily easily. I am also an accomplished artist – self-taught. I can speak 10 different languages and I can sense people's emotions. I see colours. Mind you, you would think that I would know better, but I have made some awful personal blunders in my life which still haunt me today. However, I still achieved my teaching degree. That's what I worked at. I was an art teacher in a Catholic school before I married. Married – what a mistake that was! Wrong person, wrong reasons. Wouldn't listen to advice," Dorothy trembled.

Will felt obliged to ask, "Why, what went wrong?"

"Where to start! He was a bastard to me and my kids. Control freak. He was much older than me and had been married and divorced before. The bullet lodged in the woodwork of his kitchen should have given me an inkling that all was not well. But I was young, foolish, impetuous and madly obsessed with him. He was different – never tried to impress. He was frequently rude and insulting and heartless and cold and arrogant and wealthy," she started to fill up as she reminisced about this sad time of her life.

"Why did you stay?" the obvious question.

"Remember, it was the late fifties, early sixties. It wasn't so easy then to walk away with three young children. I had no support from my parents who reckoned I had made my bed and I should lie in it. I won't go into too much detail because it hurts so much, even after all these years. You won't believe this, but to explain what kind of monster he was, when our firstborn came into the world, he told me when he finally turned up a day late, "Nice, pity it's not a boy," when the second child came, he greeted me, "Are you sure it's mine? He's far too ugly," and when my other son came, he said, "Not 3rd time lucky either." He was a pig and I couldn't wait to escape. I just didn't know how or when I would do it. Imagine a gifted, educated woman like me, allowing herself to be humiliated and belittled. I am so bitter still!" she fumed.

"Dorothy, that really is awful, how did you finally escape?"

"I took it until I could stand it no more. One day, he went to London on a business trip. I took the opportunity to pack all my possessions and my kids, and moved in with my brother who had a huge flat in Glasgow. I shall never be able to repay him. I think he saved my life or maybe from doing a life sentence. I managed somehow to get back to work as an art and language teacher. My brother never asked for anything. He allowed me to save up for a house of my own and for a good lawyer. I decided I was going to take that bastard for everything he had. I did eventually win a rather large settlement, custody and a house to buy my silence – the equivalent of an NDA. He moved down south to England. Still alive sadly!"

"Wow, that's a story and a half," Will felt her need to relate this to him. "You should write a book."

"I have often thought about it, but I wouldn't torture my kids. They were put through enough in their early lives," Dorothy said ruefully.

"How did you pick up the pieces of your life? A lone parent with three kids in the late sixties," he just had to ask.

"Well, it wasn't easy but I did it. My brother was great but I also had a great friend called Elspeth, who was also on her own after escaping from an abusive relationship. She and I supported each other. She helped mind my kids and in return, I helped her out both emotionally and spiritually. Helped her to contact her parents in the next world for reassurance. Sadly, Elspeth was killed in a RTA and that's when my life took another turn. You'll never believe what I'm going to tell you!"

"What?" said Will.

"So, before Elspeth died, we became very close and vowed that should anything ever happen to either of us, the survivor would take care of the other one's children. Elspeth left behind her only child, an 18-year-old boy, David. David was at university, studying animal medicine, when his mum passed. I took him in as he was homeless – his mum rented the house next door to me. Oh my God, I was 33 and for the next seven years, we became lovers. It was real. Just happened. We had a chemistry. I loved him and it was reciprocated. My kids, who were all under 10, loved him. We were like man and wife – but secretly. To family and friends, he was a lodger. He was so much more than that. I had never been so happy in my whole life – those seven years were fantastic and fulfilling and the best years of my life."

"How? Why did it end after those glory years?" Will was listening intently.

"He qualified as a vet and was offered a post in London. He wanted me to set up home with the kids but I couldn't do it. The timing was all wrong. My kids were just starting secondary school and were very settled. He begged me to join him but, much to my regret, I put my kids' needs first and last. Will, don't ever do that because they will get up and leave one day," Dorothy philosophised.

"Then what, Dorothy – what happened next?" Will did not know what was coming next.

"Well, I was forty-something now, three teenage kids, pressurised job, lonely, heartbroken – you can guess the rest!" Dorothy said.

"No, I can't," said Will, "I have no idea what you're going to say to me next."

"I admit, I lost the plot for quite a few years. Lost my dignity. Lost my children eventually. Lost the respect of what few friends I had. I started to drink heavily. I chased the dragon – not in the drug sense but in the love sense. I chased men, looking for the kind of love and affection and understanding and satisfaction that David gave me. I never did find anyone who came near to him in any respect, but I hurt a lot of people whilst trying to find out. I won't go into the salacious details, I'll save that for a book. I am not proud of myself, but it took me 10 years to theorise myself away from this addictive behaviour. I worked out I was the victim of adverse adult experience and positive adult experience –

my powers helped me to self-medicate and start to love myself and the world again."

"That's amazing, did you keep working while you were in gaga land?" Will commented.

"Yes, of course, I did. I spent the next few years still teaching and honing my contact with the spiritual work – did more of that. I was in my mid-fifties. Luckily, I picked up those pieces as well. I was offered redundancy. I couldn't wait. The turning point for me was when one of the pupils told me that I used to teach her granny – I thought I'm outta here. I won over the love of my children and we were all reunited – all my fault – too many uncles. I was selfish and bitter and needed love given to me. Besides that, I was gaining a well-deserved reputation for my healing work, counselling and putting people in contact with lost relatives and giving advice," Dorothy summarised.

"What sort of things were you asked to do?" Will nosily enquired.

"Mainly dealing in broken relationships and food addictions, there was a lot of smokers who wanted to give up – that sort of thing. The most lucrative part of the business is the contact with the spirit in the other world. Don't know why – because it is always up to them to contact you – you can't contact them, I had a few celebrity clients who then recommended me to other people with money to spend on this type of thing. However, as I said, I wanted to retire from this work because it takes a lot out of your body and your mind, and I am not getting any younger. I tried everything to put them off – overcharging, but still they come. My God, my chips are getting cold – can I blether?" she said.

"You sure can," joked Will, "I haven't spoken to you for nine months – I didn't want to interrupt."

"Oh my God, Will, what will you think of me. I have told you far too much and I don't even really know you that well," Dorothy seemed slightly alarmed

"Don't worry, Dorothy, I am not here to judge you. I'm here to buy you a McDonalds."

70

"Will we meet again? I have loved talking to you," Dorothy confided.

"Of course, I'll call you again," Will said goodbye.

"Oh! By the way, I have a message for you from Ellen and Matt. They told me to tell you that they are both fine. Keep up the writing and your beautiful dreams will come true," she said nonchalantly.

Will thought, *I definitely have to see her again. How could she know my parents' names…?*

I Met an Angel

Richie left the house, banging the front door as loudly as he could. He had just finished yet another angry exchange with Jackie, his torn-faced wife. Once again, she had embarrassed him in front of his group of friends at a night out. She was drunk and had fallen asleep in the toilet in the middle of a noisy cabaret. He had to get some totally random woman to fetch her out of the loo. She made the usual excuses that she was stressed and depressed. Richie had had enough of her. The only reason for her behaviour, as far as he could see, was that she had necked a full bottle of wine in a short space of time, prior to them leaving for their outing. He could no longer accept her apologies and decided to get out of her way before he did something he would later regret – he was so angry. He needed space to sort out in his mind what he was going to do about her.

He was walking along the busy, main street deciding where to walk to. He thought it best to do a little comfort shopping in the nearby supermarket – buying things always seemed to soothe his mood. As he strode towards the route to the shop, he saw a blonde woman sauntering towards him. She looked bewildered, stunned and possibly inebriated. He thought to himself, *Is she staggering or is she, maybe, ill?*

As he got nearer to her, he could see that she was upset and crying and distressed. His compassion could not let him ignore her – he had to ask:

"Are you all right? Pet, you seem a bit nonplussed."

"No, I am not all right!" she said, "My husband has just thrown me out of my own house. I have nowhere to go!"

He could tell she was drunk. It was only around eleven o'clock on a Saturday morning. He had just left a drunk in the house, but he still couldn't just walk away.

"Why has your husband done this to you?" he asked.

"I've been drinking for five weeks solidly since my father died. He was eighty-five. I am a nurse, I should know better but I just can't get over it. I know he's in a better place. I just feel so sad," she cried.

Richie put his arms round her shoulder. He could see that she needed comforting.

"What do you expect your hubby to do after five weeks of drunkenness? Are you not surprised it has taken him so long to get fed up with you?"

"I suppose so," she mumbled.

"Look," he said empathetically, "do you really think your old dad would like to see you like this? Of course, he wouldn't. You probably made him the proudest dad in the world with all your achievements. I hope my daughter would turn out as good as you. Come on – you're a nurse, you know what harm you are doing to yourself and your family. Stop drinking. Go home. Get help. Please!"

The stranger was stunned at his straightforwardness. She hugged him and kissed him on the cheek. She asked if he was married.

"When you go home, tell your wife she is a lucky woman. Tell her, I think I met an angel."

Richie smiled, "I'm no angel – no one is."

They went their separate ways. Richie hoped she would be all right, but didn't want to take her home to her already irate husband. He wondered what she would do and thought of the whole conversation as quite a spiritual experience. He did not know why he stopped. He did not know why two strangers communicated in the way they did. He carried on his journey and bought some comfort food before returning to the hostile atmosphere in his house. The next day, he had built a bridge in his mind and had crossed over it. All was forgiven until the next time.

Six months later, Richie was again taking his daily exercise which involved a walk to his local park, and then a stop for a coffee and a short shop in his local supermarket. He was wheeling round with his trolley looking for 'whoopsies' when he stumbled across the same drunk woman he had comforted earlier. She immediately recognised him and he her. She looked considerably better than she had when they first met. Richie thought about not doing anything – no reaction but Ann-Marie approached him first.

"Hi there!" she said, "Do you remember me?"

"Yes, of course, but I can't remember getting your name!"

"I'm Ann-Marie. I just needed to tell you how much you helped me. You'll never know what you did for me. I will never forget your words or your kindness! As you can see, I am back in the land of the living – sorry, I never even asked your name."

"I'm Richie."

Her words, *I think I met an angel*, resonated in his mind.

Marylyn

It is often difficult to find a discernible link highlighting the effects of political decisions upon the livelihoods of ordinary people. However, it is clear to me that Thatcher's decision to disintegrate Britain's manufacturing base, during the early 1980s, divested vast swathes of the country – not least Glasgow's East End, where factory after factory was closed down, rendering the employees defenceless and unable to change their situation. Marylyn's parents, Noel and Marion, both worked at Templeton Carpets as weavers and both were simultaneously made redundant. A curse neither fully recovered from.

There they were settled nicely with their two kids, Marylyn and Ronnie, living in an apartment in Bridgeton. They had been saving up their hard-earned cash for a deposit on a brand-new house. Marion's mum watched the two kids whilst their parents worked. From the day the factory manager announced that the business was to close, life seemed to be on a downward spiral.

That happened in July 1981. Three years later, there was no change – still unemployed and frustrated with their existence. It wasn't all bad though, occasionally Marion used to be able to get some casual cleaning work in Pollokshields to supplement their benefit income. They were getting by – just.

Therefore, it made it all the more inexplicable why Noel decided during the Orange Walk in Bridgeton to break through the parade lines. Did he have a death wish? Why would he attempt to get to the other side of the road through the marchers? It wasn't as though he was unfamiliar with the culture coming from Newry (albeit the opposite side) and he had lived in Glasgow for some time, mostly in the hotbed of sectarianism that was Bridgeton. It was no surprise that he failed to reach the other side without being booted, trampled on and left for dead. In fact, he did not die straightaway. He was taken to the Royal Infirmary, where it was confirmed that he died from the injuries he sustained, four days later.

Marion, at twenty-five years old was a shell-shocked widow left with two children under five. She received no answers to her questions. What had happened to her husband? How did he get from Main St, Bridgeton to the banks of the River Clyde at Dalmarnock? No witnesses! No justice! No charges! No exhaustive investigation! Just an unexplained death. The police, it appeared, were tied up with duties at Orgreave, helping their colleagues defeat the miners. The local constabulary were undermanned. There were quite a few incidents throughout the city. Noel's departure was just one of them. She was bemused, numb and defeated. All that was left of Noel was a blood-stained, cracked watch and a pile of clothes taken from him when he was admitted to the hospital. She could only think of how she could protect and shield her children. She could see only as far as one day at a time.

The next few years, Marion brought Marylyn and Ronnie up the best way she knew how. They both progressed through nursery, then primary school. They were not treated like other children. They were only allowed out to the park supervised by herself. They were never allowed to have friends into the house, never allowed to join clubs (mainly for fiscal rather than social reasons), never allowed out to play on their own or develop hobbies. The two kids weren't treated badly. Marion looked after them meticulously and kept them immaculately clean. Their home was clean and well-kept. Marion ran a tight ship to the exclusion of everyone else, refusing even family support. The family was regarded as anti-social. Marion didn't care what people or neighbours thought of her, as far as she was concerned, she was doing her duty.

The way they lived, remained unchanged until the kids reached the teenage stage. Marylyn was all right. She was a home bird who was quite content to stay in with her mum as long as she could get her weekly copy of the *Jackie* and was allowed to decorate her room with pictures of the latest pop stars. She was given the occasional new item of clothing or a new single. Marylyn was docile. She just wanted a small amount of luxury – no big demands or rebellion. She passed through school with an unremarkable academic record or without any obvious charisma or personality. She was a harmless dormouse. Marion liked it that way. Ronnie, on the other hand, was a different animal from the very start of the teenage years.

He began to rebel against the house regime. He was boisterous. He wanted to be out in the community to be with his peers. He was a boy, a bad boy. His behaviour was disruptive whenever he attended school (which was not often), he joined the local gang and became territorially aggressive against anyone not from Bridgeton. He started to smoke cannabis when he was thirteen, drank with teenagers older than he was and gradually became an active petty criminal as he advanced through his teenage years. He went through the process from 'Children's Panel' to 'Young Offender' with predictable inevitability. He was largely out of Marion's control. He was largely out of his own control as he descended into a chaotic lifestyle to feed his growing addictions to alcohol and drugs. Realistically, she was relieved when he was finally incarcerated when his crimes were finally brought to account. At least, she knew where he was.

She and Marylyn continued with their mundane lives. Marion rarely ventured out other than to shop or buy booze from the local off-licence. Marylyn left school. She had been encouraged to try several YTS schemes in an attempt to get her to think about how she would sustain herself in the future. But Marylyn's mind-set did not allow her to think that way. Nothing lasted more than a day. She tried retail, hospitality, catering – nothing worked for her. She preferred to be at home with her mum. She never felt that she fitted in anywhere else. Her life centred on her bedroom. Her existence was getting up in the morning – her mum would make her breakfast. They would tidy up the house. They would go shopping. Marylyn would go to her bedroom to read – her mum would make their lunch. They would watch an old movie in the afternoon and maybe have a few vodkas – her mum would then make their evening meal. They would watch television whilst having a few drinks each night. This routine went on for years, then when Marylyn was 19, she made a bid for freedom and applied for a house of her own. Marylyn managed to get her own council flat close to her mother's house. The only difference to her lifestyle was that her mum had arranged for all her bills to be deducted directly from her benefit to all the main utility and housing organisations. Marylyn and her carried on with the same routine except that at night, Marylyn went home and slept in her own house.

Marylyn's life changed abruptly when one morning, as per usual, she shoved on her housecoat, put her clothes in a bag and made her pyjama-clad way to her mum's house for breakfast. She pressed the doorbell – no reply, she rattled the letterbox – nothing, she looked through the letterbox and called her mum – not a sound. This was so unusual. She immediately sensed something was wrong. Her instincts were found to be correct. Marylyn went back to her own house and picked up the spare house keys. She opened the door with great trepidation. She found her mother lying dead on the floor in her bedroom. The post mortem showed that she had suffered an aneurism and had died earlier that morning. Marylyn was in total shock. She didn't really know what to do. She called the police and an ambulance. The police basically had to tell her all the processes that needed to be followed, and a kind lady from the job centre helped her to complete all the forms she needed to report the death and to get help to pay for the funeral.

The funeral itself was a really sad affair. The only witnesses were Marylyn, her brother, Ronnie, and a friend he had met from prison called Ralph as well as the priest and the undertaker. All the rest of the people in the chapel were just attending Mass as normal. After the cremation, Marylyn, her brother and Ralph went to the pub to drown their sorrows.

They were only there for a short time when Ronnie left her alone with his friend whilst he went off in pursuit of a hit. Ralph was a player. He took advantage of Marylyn's vulnerability. Before too long, after an appropriate amount of sympathy, affection, empathy and alcohol, they went to back to Marylyn's flat. It was ironic that the first time that she had slept with a man was on the same day she cremated her mother. She knew it was kind of wrong because he did tell her he was married, but she needed love and to be told she was loved. Marylyn kept the affair with Ralph going for a few weeks. She knew she was being used but it suited her. He only ever turned up at her door in early evening. He never took her anywhere. Just brought her drinks and expected sex in return, then he would leave after he achieved his objective. Marylyn drew a halt to the affair, if you could call it that, when he started to suggest that she should come and meet his wife. She knew what he was implying. He was not very subtle about it. He had crossed her line. When Marylyn rejected his suggestions, Ralph exacted a horrible revenge on her. He spread rumours around the locality that she was an insatiable whore who would do anything with anybody at any time. He daubed offensive spray painting on her front door. He let anyone, who would listen, know what he had been allowed to do to her. He totally besmirched her reputation in what was a small world. Marylyn was oblivious to the assertions. She substituted his affections by purchasing a small dog, which she called Rocky.

The next few months were very cruel to Marylyn. Her health deteriorated as she did not look after herself properly. She was mentally low all the time and physically, she was losing weight through not feeding herself. She existed on pot noodles. Her only exercise was looking after her dog. Matters really came to a head one night when her brother came to her door. He had been goaded by his friend's childish jibes – he couldn't get those words out of his mind. Marylyn was really uptight. He was clearly agitated and high on a cocktail of drugs. He started to verbally abuse her. He told her everyone in Bridgeton knew she was a slut. He told her Ralph had described how she performed on him. He started to go mad and threatened to rape her. Marylyn was frantic with fear. He rag-dolled her through to the bedroom. He was pulling her by the hair. She screamed as loudly as she could. Somehow, she scrambled out of the bedroom and out of the house. She thought he was going to kill her. She roused a neighbour who called the police. During the time they took to arrive on the scene, he ransacked and vandalised her whole house. He slashed her leather suite, smashed all her crockery, threw all her clothes out of the window and emptied all her foodstuff over the floor. The police entered the building and arrested him. He was later sectioned and placed in Leverndale Psychiatric Unit where he remains to this day. Marylyn's life was in total disarray. No hope, no job, no future, no friends – just despair and desolation.

One morning, Marylyn was out walking her dog on Glasgow Green when she met Sandra Barr. Sandra was an employment adviser with Jobs and Business Glasgow. She had dealings with Marylyn previously through work. She was unable to help her, mainly due to the fact that, although she was a nice enough kid, she had no concept of sustaining her own life. Sandra always felt that there was something holding Marylyn back from participating in normal teenage activities. She didn't know why but she felt sorry for Marylyn. It was her innocence and vulnerability that made her so needy. However, Sandra was really shocked when she saw the state Marylyn was in. She was so thin and emaciated. She had gone from being slightly larger than delightfully plump to a skinny rake with her cheekbones prominent in her face, and her collarbone highlighting her shrivelled frame.

Sandra felt she couldn't just walk by. She asked her if she was all right – knowing full well she wasn't. She invited Marylyn round to the community centre where she was going for a coffee.

"What's happening to you, Marylyn? You don't look well at all."

Marylyn then began to tell Sandra of the hellish things that had happened to her since her mum had died so unexpectedly, and the personal battles she had gone through physically and mentally. Sandra lived locally and she had heard the story about her brother and his friend. Sandra befriended Marylyn. Marylyn was so grateful that she had someone to trust. Sandra, then, introduced Marylyn to a lady who worked in the community centre called Sally Park. Sally was a real livewire who made it her life's work to cheer people up and help people in her local community. She ran all sorts of classes in confidence building, cookery, well-being, employability, handicrafts and computer classes. Sally was the breath of fresh air and new life that Marylyn needed. Sally became like a surrogate mother to Marylyn in a short space of time. She did not allow Marylyn to wallow in self-pity, instead she forced her to do things for herself. She persuaded her to go to a bereavement counsellor – even taking the time out to go with her for support. This proved to be really beneficial as Marylyn was able to release her feelings and let go of the past. She still held on to her father's watch. She had previously thought about resurrecting a cold case with the police. However, after careful consideration, she felt the only way she could move forward was by leaving the past behind. Sally was instrumental in allowing Marylyn to make decisions for herself.

Sally engaged Marylyn in voluntary work at the centre. She taught her to cook and cater for the local pensioners. This was major progress for Marylyn and had to be started from point zero. How to use a microwave, peel potatoes, boil pasta, make toast, fry an egg – all experiments which Marylyn had never tried to do before. Her confidence grew; she was a real star in the centre. All the pensioners and kids knew her. She used to prepare food and the hall for all the local functions. She began to develop her cooking skills and could competently make a three-course meal for up to fifty people. She began to look after herself properly. Her life really took an upswing when she applied for a nursing auxiliary job at the Southern General. She didn't really expect to get the job as she was now 26 and had never actually been employed before.

However, her references and the charisma and personality she displayed at her first interview, convinced NHS ward sister to give her a chance.

This was a life-changing break for Marylyn. She thrived in the pressurised environment of helping people. She felt like a member of the human race for the first time in her life. She no longer had to rely on benefit to support herself. She was independent and proud. She loved what she was doing; she didn't look for progress. She was content with her lot. Another bonus was that, after a few months of working in the hospital, she met a chirpy hospital porter called Willie Wilson. Willie asked her to go out with him. A romance soon blossomed. Willie asked her to marry and she accepted his offer. She moved out of Bridgeton, for the first time in her life, to Glasgow Southside. The couple then had two children in quick succession. Marylyn recalled her own childhood and was determined that her own kids would have every opportunity she and her husband could give them. Those kids tried everything from Irish dancing to karate. She made sure they would enjoy their lives and that she would live hers.

No Strings Attached

Jeni arrived home from work at six o'clock. Her kids, Amy and Jack, were engrossed in their computer. She asked them what they were doing, thinking it might have been something to do with homework. Alas no! They were talking to their friends on www.teenchat.com.

She asked them to get off the computer and help her to prepare the evening meal. Jeni had endured a hard day at work. Her boss had asked her to analyse why her team had failed to reach its target and she was exhausted by her own efforts. She was finding life tough since she and her partner had separated a year ago. She felt the kids were taking her for granted and not taking their share of the domestics. She chided them, but not strongly. It wasn't their fault that their dad had left home or that she was stressed out by work.

Jeni made their meal and the teenagers shared the cleaning up. Jeni insisted they finish their homework before going near the computer. The kids went back online. She could hear them cackling and was glad they, at least, were happy. She herself had settled down to her normal routine of reading over her notes from work, then settling down to a humdrum night in front of the television. She had tried to resurrect her social life but without much success. Most of her friends were couples and had children to look after. She had tried singles clubs but it was either the wrong time, wrong place, wrong mood or the wrong man. She had grown used to staying in. She even made excuses to herself so she wouldn't ask her mum to watch the kids. Amy and Jack were teenagers now, they had their own social scene and really only required her to finance it.

At 10 o'clock, as usual, she made sure the kids had gone to bed or were, at least, confined to their rooms. Normally, she would just have gone to bed soon after the kids, but on this particular evening she didn't feel tired. She sat down at the computer desk and started to check out which sites those kids were using. She satisfied herself that the firewall was effective and nothing untoward was happening. She began to wander what these chat lines were all about. Her curiosity was based around the fun the kids seemed to have and the ennui of her own life.

She reflected that she wished she had had more fun as a teenager. She knew she has wasted her youth. She had met her husband, Andy, when she was sixteen, she became pregnant, and they married and started their family when they were still children themselves. She had had to grow up too fast. She had managed to get her career back on track in recent years, however, her marriage had gone pear-shaped. Jeni had no bad feeling against Andy, after all, he was the only man she had ever had, he was the father of their children and he was a decent man – but she had simply outgrown him.

Jeni poured herself a drink. She was tempted to go online. The youngsters in her office were always talking about it, she was bored, she was boring and she needed something to occupy her time. She went onto Google and discovered nsa.com. She gingerly typed in her details and soon attracted a response. It came from a man called Kev.

"How are you tonight, Jeni?"
"Not bad, thanks, I'm a first-time user on site. You'll need to help me, Kev."
"That's not a problem, I'll show you the way. What's your take on the music scene? Like modern or what? What books you into? Enjoy clubbing? Driving? Hols what?"

"70s and 80s my era. Love Bee Gees, Donna Summer and Human League. Don't read much – no time! Love sun from wherever, can drive, prefer not to. Are clubs not still called discos? Great singer, adore karaoke," Jeni sent her message without inhibition, she poured another drink.

"Wow! I don't believe it. How MUCH have we got in common? I love all that. 'Don't You Want Me Baby' and all that. I sing at every opportunity too! Great letting your inhibitions go at a night out – nothing better. Nice to chat, contact you later. Be a good girl!"

"Night, night, Kev."

Jeni couldn't believe how casual and relaxed she had been with this stranger. She was normally not quiet, but reserved. All those open questions. Why had she told him so much about herself in two brief conversations? It must have been the drink or maybe she was beginning to lighten up. She didn't know but she could hardly suppress her excitement at the idea of someone actually being interested in what she liked and how she felt. That felt good.

The next night when the kids had gone to bed, she checked her message box. Kev had been in touch. She didn't hesitate to reply.

"Kev, it's me. Finally, on me-time. Kids in bed. What you been up to today?"

"Busy! Busy! Busy! Manager of a new club! Trying to find suitable staff! Very difficult at present, probably have to break a few rules and employ some willing Poles! Yourself?"

"I, too, stressed at work. I think I might go on the sick. Frightened of the sack though. Just cheering myself up, having a wee drink and listening to CDs. Wouldn't have a job for me, would you?"

"No, Jeni, you're far too clever for this line of work. Cleaning, waitressing – you're too good from what I can make out. I'm listening to Rod Stewart just now, d'you like him?"

"Nah! More of a George Michael kind of girl, me! You know, romantic and passionate."

"Yes, you sound it. But are you boasting or are you as passionate as you say!"

"That's for you to find out."

"Why don't I, then?"

The chat was very direct. They exchanged lots of sexual innuendo, banter, coaxing, goading, teasing and daring to see how far the other would go. They arranged to meet two days later at the Travel Inn, Glasgow City Centre. Jeni immediately began to worry as soon as she had made the arrangement. She'd never slept with anyone bar her husband! Yet, two days later, she was about to meet a man she had never seen before as a result of a cyber-conversation. She did not contact him the next day. She could not make up her mind whether or not to keep the appointment. She swithered. She had never before been promiscuous. What was she doing? Trying to recapture her missing youth. What had she got to lose? What harm was in it? She convinced herself it was OK, and she met Kev the next day.

Both of them arrived at the guesthouse on time. She recognised him from his profile, he smiled at her. They had a quick, introductory drink at the bar before checking into the room. He was confident and nonchalant, she was nervous. They took off their clothes and went to the bed (I will spare you the heaving body stage because the story is not about that) and their bodies heaved. She felt relief and satisfaction. He was empowered.

"I'll have to go soon, Jeni. I've got to pick up the kids from school, then I've got a very important meeting. Thanks for this afternoon," he said coldly.

"Yeh, Kev, will we see each other again?" Jeni muttered apologetically.

"Jeni, no strings attached."

Jeni went home. She found it difficult to get over what she had just done. She was disappointed because she knew the score. She had hoped that this encounter might have led to a real relationship. Later that night, she tried to contact Kev on nsa.com. He did not reply to her messages. She was devastated and liberated all at the same time. She reconciled her thoughts by making herself believe that her behaviour was cool and trendy. She knew she would try the site again. She was hooked on the thrill.

The next day, she went onto nsa.com again. There was a message for her. Was it Kev? NO. It was another guy in his thirties called Rob, making enquiries. Jeni responded immediately.

"Hi, Rob, how's it going? Received your message."
"Jeni, viewed your profile, you sound nice. How's the singing going?"
"Still warbling."

Jeni engaged in conversation so easily on the computer. She knew that before she would even dream of singing in public, she would have needed a right few G&Ts, yet, here she was, exuding confidence and ebullience with guys she never seen. She loved the flattery, attention, the freedom to do as she pleased, the power at her fingertips and the sheer enjoyment that had eluded her during her earlier years.

A similar pattern to the first relationship/encounter followed. First, the flattery, the brinksmanship in pattoir, the illicit meeting and then, nothing. Jeni was conscious that she was becoming addicted to the chat line. It boosted her ego as a woman that these suitors wanted to chat. Her personality changed recognisably. Initially, she joined the gym to tone up, then it was tattoos, which increased in size and consequentiality. She even considered piercings in public and private places, but she still had to retain some integrity and respectability. She became aware of her hedonistic attitude but this clashed with the need not to embarrass her children. She really didn't care what most people thought but she still managed to keep a lid on her emotions whilst enjoying her alter ego. Six months ago, she had been a one-man woman, now she was looking at double figures. She still hadn't met anyone on a permanent basis and all the lovers vanished after one escapade. She was beginning to doubt her ability to sustain a relationship, but told herself that this was normal in the modern world. All her friends were wondering what was happening to Jeni. She had gone from Mrs Right to Mrs Right-Now, despite her efforts to shield her secret life and never,

ever discussing her activities. She knew she would be demonised, as it was, she was the talk of the steamie. The visible changes in her appearance made her the subject of some conjecture, however, she reigned herself in as to her inner emotions and kept her hidden attractions well under wraps. In the last six months, she'd been with a plumber, two electricians, a bricklayer, a foreman and a quantity surveyor. She had built up a good knowledge of the construction sector within a short period of time.

Then, one quiet Sunday morning, Jeni got the shock of her life. She opened up her Sunday Mail to read the headline, 'COUNCILLOR IN SWINGERS CLUB SCANDAL'. The article was about a vice ring which had been formed from an internet site nsa.com. The story revealed that a group of councillors had opened up a swinger's club in Glasgow's West End called 'NO STRINGS ATTACHED', and the premises had gained a license for entertainment and alcohol through the club owner who happened to be on the council committee, approving the opening of the club. The usual suspects frequented it: footballers, judges, MPs, priests and ministers. The photographs accompanying the article showed faces of the six main protagonists involved in the club. Jeni was horrified. She knew them all. Not by the names that were in the paper, but she knew it was them. Jeni freaked out, the paper said these men and the nsa.com site were about to be investigated. What did this mean for her? What if the policed tracked her activities on this site? What if she was implicated in any wrongdoing? What if her face was in the paper? What if her kids, her mum and family found out? She thought, *God, these bastards have passed me on like a piece of meat! How else would they know how to press the right buttons to get me going? What a fool!*

After an hour or so, she calmed herself by persuading herself that she had done nothing wrong. It was no one else's business and the police would never contact her. Jeni was never contacted.

The next day, after the newspaper article, Jeni went into work as usual. Her computer beeped, *'You have an email'*, she opened it. The message was from Tony, who worked in her team. The message read:

"Hi, Jeni, let's do lunch."

She thought for a second, *At least I know this one*, she replied.

"OK."

At the lunch, Tony confessed that he had been admiring her from a distance for some time and wanted to ask her out to dine. Jeni was subjected to a total charm offensive that she could not resist. At last, she was able to nurture and develop a relationship with a real person. She was going to confess what had happened to her, but then decided there were no strings attached.

NSA.com: No Strings Attached

I know a club called NSA,
For men and women, straight and gay,
It's for the unattached and alone,
To service one another from the phone.

You don't need an excuse or a pretext,
Just place your order for uncommitted sex,
You don't need any cash in hand,
Or someone to judge or understand.

The pleasure gained is for a short while,
It's the latest fad, an empty style,
You don't need to know each other's name,
As long as your needs are both the same.

A soulless exchange of physical wares,
No one to judge, no one who cares,
You join the crew, you take your chance,
But whatever happened to love and romance.

There's something missing, it's not human,
For all the lonely people, men and women,
Who meets a geek through the internet?
Only out for any pleasure they can get.

This is cyber love, it cannot fail,
To find what you are looking for from email,
Say what you like, call me a cynic,
But it'll lengthen the queue at the clinic.

It's not success or remotely cool,
To sleep with strangers as a rule,
There's something real about personality and charm,
Meet someone with both, you won't come to harm.

There are many ways for humans to meet,
Methods to sweep each other off our feet,
Tell me, Lord, it's not too late,
To move one step up from the speed date.

Profiles

Grace was fed-up with her mundane life. Work to home, home to work every day – nothing else – no social life, no fun and still lonely. She had split up with her partner over three years ago but still hadn't moved on. She was fair, fat, forty and far from happy. She continued to live in the past, often questioning as to where it had all gone wrong her. She used to have drive, ambition and assertiveness in her persona. She convinced herself that the reason for her situation was that she had those qualities in abundance – that's why he left her. Her mind-set, however, was transformed. She purchased an inspirational self-help on how to improve life through positive thinking. She didn't really know if it was indeed the book or just that her psyche had changed. All she knew was that she was ready to move on.

She started the process by joining her local gym, joining a local slimming group and a local walking club. She persevered with these changes and the effects were quite dramatic. She lost 12 stone, gained a new confidence and a few new friendships within a relatively short space of time. She was still lonely as most of the people she associated with were mainly people of different generations – either too young or too old. She didn't seem to be able to meet anyone in her own age group. She tried singles nights, speed dating and a few recommendations but without success. She tried to refrain from using internet-dating sites, as she had heard so many traumatic stories, however, frustration finally overcame her and she decided to go for it.

Having tried a few free ones, which proved fruitless and full of filthy nutters, she decided to use a professional site which specialised in people who worked in caring professions as she did. She completed her profile, describing herself as energetic, lonely, looking for a permanent relationship, athletic and fun. She revealed her interests as going to the gym and watching movies. She waited patiently for responses. A few hours later, one duly arrived.

Harold described himself as a kind, caring, compassionate, empathetic man, who loved entertaining and cooking. He said he would like to meet the woman of his dreams.

She was interested. They both started to gently flirt with each other but not in the crude way the free site participants did. There was no innuendo, just gentle banter. The conversation ended with an invitation from Harry to Grace to come over to his house for dinner the next day. He promised the best Indian food he could make and that she had ever tasted. He said he would make it a night to remember, she would never forget it – he got that bit right.

Grace was excited and thought how nice that was for someone to go to the trouble of making a meal for her. She spent the night thinking about how to dress to impress, how to control her emotions and avoiding appearing too keen. She woke that morning feeling slightly uncomfortable and had a stomach-ache. She put it down to indigestion but as the day wore on, she did feel a little queasier. She was swithering whether or not to cancel the date. She was so looking forward to meeting this guy who seemed like the best prospect she had for years. She prepared an overnight bag just in case, but decided to leave it in the car so as not to be so suggestive. She put on her best outfit, took another indigestion tablet and set off for his house which was situated in a rather posh suburb in Glasgow. She was feeling a bit iffy, maybe even slightly nauseous, but put it down to a combination of nerves and excitement.

She arrived at his house a little earlier than arranged. She had caught him unawares. He was preparing the food and was wearing a plastic pinnie with only his blue, silk boxer shorts underneath. He invited her in and told her to wait in the lounge while he got dressed. The house was beautiful. Very tasteful.

The aroma of food pervaded over the whole room. He came down into the lounge fully clothed. He was a smart dresser she thought – very upmarket, especially the shoes. He asked her what she wanted to drink. She opted for soft as she had still to drive home (maybe) and she also still felt quite unwell. She was trying not to let her discomfort show as she did not want anything to spoil the evening. He left her in the lounge and went to prepare the starters for them.

He called her through to the dining area. The table was set out beautifully. She could tell he was classy – it fitted his profile. He brought out homemade pakoras, pompadoms, spiced onions and samosas to start with. The food was presented perfectly and it smelt lovely. She nibbled away as they made polite conversation. All the time, her stomach was becoming more and more painful but she was thinking she would persevere, make her excuses and leave early. She did not want to offend him as he had clearly gone to a lot of expense and trouble to make her date an enjoyable one. He had even bought her flowers, what more could a girl ask for. They finished the starters and he took the plates to the kitchen. He brought out the next course, a huge tureen full of chicken tikka masala. He also provided a massive bowl full of rice. He invited Grace to help herself to the food. She took quite a large quantity of rice and chicken and covered the rice with sauce. Harold forgot to bring hand towels and returned to the kitchen to get them. When he got back into the dining room, he found Grace's face down slumped in the chicken tikka masala plate. As he entered the room, all he could see was the orange sauce stuck to her face and dripping off her hair. Assuming she was drunk, he flew into a rage. He was clearly thinking he had met another Weegie steamer (a drunk Glaswegian woman).

"How dare you come to my house in that state? Get out my sight!" he screamed at her.

Grace was in so much pain, she could not explain herself to him. She staggered to her car and immediately drove to the A&E near where she lived. She was examined by a doctor who immediately diagnosed appendicitis. Her appendix had to be removed as soon as possible. She thought how handy that overnight bag was. She was in agony and all she could think was that her date certainly did not match his profile. What happened to Mr Nice, Kind and Considerate?

The next thing Grace remembered, was being knocked out by the anaesthetic and waking up in a high-dependency ward in the hospital. She could imagine herself floating up towards a bright light and, for a brief moment, thought she might be dead, she was having an out of body experience. She was then awoken by the nurse who had attended to her all through the night. The nurse kept talking to her, just to keep her awake. She explained the registrar would come round later when she was feeling up to it, to explain what procedure was carried out and what the next stage was. She drifted in and out of consciousness for the rest of the morning. She still hadn't even contacted anyone to let them know of her ordeal – goodness only knows how she signed the consent forms, she thought. The morning passed and as lunchtime approached, the nursing team tried to coax her to sit up, so she could have her lunch.

Later that day, as she was beginning to revive and attempting to sort out the sequence of events in her mind, there was a knock on her room door. The registrar was doing his round to evaluate all the post-operative patients. There he was, Dr Harold Webster, her date night disaster. She recognised him straightaway and he her. She still had the remnants of his chicken tikka masala stuck to her head. He had to decide whether to acknowledge her personally or not. He mulled over her notes and was able to see that she must have been in acute pain and not drunk as he had surmised. He asked the nurse to go and find notes for another patient at the nurse's station, to buy some time to be with Grace on his own.

"My God, Grace, I am so sorry. How can I ever make it up to you? Please forgive me. I just jumped to the wrong conclusion. I am so sorry!" he apologised for his pathetic behaviour.

"Yes, sure," she said quietly, "you should be ashamed of the way you treated me!"

"I am – please forgive me. Please let's start again when you have recovered," his face reddened with embarrassment.

"We'll see," Grace said firmly.

The doctor kept tabs on her recuperation and when she was about to be discharged, he approached her again.

"Look! That night, that was not me. Please let me show you the real me. Phone me or send an email if you can bring yourself to delete that trauma I put you through!"

A few weeks later, Grace decided to give him the benefit of the doubt. She called him and arranged another date night – this time on neutral territory. He charmed his way back into her life and eventually she moved in with him, but every now again when she needs some emotional leverage, she raises the issue of how he left her for dead, the events of that first date night grew arms and legs as the years wore on. He still cringes when he thinks of what an idiot he was, but she has made him pay big time for his mistake. Revenge is sweet.

Suddenly – The Kiss

He never thought it would have been like it was. He had always imagined himself to be the devoted, sensible, straight as a die, faithful boyfriend. He found himself challenged and he failed.

His friend's girlfriend was drunk. She propositioned him. He resisted. I think the words were:

"Behave yourself, you!!!"

Then, she kissed him and his whole set of rules and values were blown away. He responded too well and felt so guilty at the pleasure he derived. He had to unburden himself from the guilt, his betrayal.

So he called Rick, another friend, he just had to tell someone. He related the story, seeking absolution. He implored:

"It wasn't just my fault. I didn't instigate it. I did openly resist the temptation until the kiss."

"What do you mean THE kiss? A kiss is just a kiss," said Rick, a man without vast experience, but a good listener.

"It was incredible. So succulent and passionate. Made the hairs on my back stand on end with excitement. I forgot all my loyalty to Simon. I didn't even think of HIS feelings, once she kissed me, I felt passion like I never did before. I never wanted that electric feeling to go away. The tingle of her tongue as she teased me! I wanted to stop it but my body was responding. My heart was palpitating. It was wrong but it felt so right. The saliva mixing. The taste of her lipstick. The fact that she obviously fancied me. What a thrill! Should I tell someone else? Will you promise not to tell anyone else?"

"That must have been some kiss!"

The Best Jockey

If ever anyone had a chance of leaving behind the drudgery of a rundown council estate in South Glasgow called Arden, it was a little toe rag named Stuart Munro. In its fifty-year history, Arden was notorious for breeding vandalism; Eddi Reader and a Channel 5 mockumentary starring Colin and Justin, highlighting the worst element of the scheme.

His life of crime started at a very early age. He had this overwhelming need to be part of the underworld. No one really understood why, especially his family, who were hard-working, proud people who did everything they could for their children. His parents were one of the few families on the estate who had a car; both parents worked and their children were always dressed in the best of gear. They thought, perhaps, the reason for his behaviour was that he was small. Maybe, he was trying to compensate for his lack of stature by involving himself with dangerous tasks set out for him by the local neds.

Stuart was always up to no good. He was always the one who used his tiny frame to gain access to places he had no right to be. At first, when he was caught red-handed in the legal newsagents, long after closing time, people blamed other older kids for putting him up to mischief. Believe you me, he needed no encouragement at all. He loved the thrill of theft. He loved being involved with the in-crowd, the bad ones. He was an out-and-out rogue. Not violent, just simply a thief who did not show the slightest remorse for his actions. He would break into shops, offices, factories and if required by those he sought to favour, rich peoples' houses. He would sell the proceeds to anyone who would buy – where he came from, there was always a ready market. He loved money. He couldn't get enough of it. No matter what his parents gave him, he always had the urge to get more, always illegally and always to be part of the crowd.

By the time he was thirteen, he was quite an accomplished wrongdoer. He was a truant who didn't see why it was wrong for him not to go to school. His personal crime wave was in its third year and he had still not been brought to account. He managed to dodge the long arm of the law because he was so young and could not be charged or caught; however, it was his continued absence from school that brought him to the attention of the authorities.

Stuart, accompanied by his then frantic parents, was placed before the children's panel and a social worker was appointed to help him get his life back on track and to support his parents.

Graham was the social worker assigned to help Stuart. Graham and Stuart hit it off straightaway. Graham himself was once an Arden boy, so he knew the type of environment the boy lived in. He felt he had to move him away from his cronies if there was to be any chance to move forward. He had a flash of inspiration. Graham suggested to the boy, due to his size and weight, he might consider a career as a jockey. Stuart was very responsive and Graham arranged for him, as part of his rehabilitation, to undertake riding lessons at a school in Ayrshire, near to where he lived in Kilmaurs and just far enough away from Glasgow.

Stuart realising that he needed a way out of his criminal lifestyle, put his heart and soul into the training. Prior to going to the farm, he had never seen a horse close-up. The nearest he'd been to was one was at a football match, where he saw police horses. He never really approached them due to his aversion to the constabulary. Stuart was a natural. He grew to love the animals; they seemed to reciprocate. He learned how to walk, trot, gallop and jump fences. The bit he didn't like was cleaning the stables. At last, he was happy. He seemed to have a purpose in life. Graham, in consultation with the lad's family, progressed to the next stage of his plan. He helped him compose a letter which was to be sent to all the racing stable yards in Scotland and Northern England, to ask if he could seek employment as an apprentice jockey. He had all the right attributes even though he was from an urban background. He was an ideal size and weight at under seven stones, he could ride out and was familiar with all the tasks a stable lad might be expected to perform. He wrote to the yards in Ayr, Hamilton, Musselburgh, Perth, Kelso as well as far down south as Yorkshire.

Much to Stuart's surprise and delight, his letter prompted a good response. He was invited for an interview to a yard at Ayr racecourse, run by a very successful Scottish trainer called Craig Bell. The trainer had contacted his friend, who ran the training school in Kilmaurs that Stuart had attended. Craig heard good reports about the young Glaswegian and invited him down for a trial. The trainer was impressed by his attitude and determination to succeed. He offered the boy a position as a stable lad in the yard. He was delighted to accept his offer.

Stuart quickly found out how much hard work and preparation was required to run a racing yard, His wages were so low, a meagre ten pounds per week, plus his keep. He was up at five in the morning, six days a week. Before he even had the opportunity to ride the racehorses, he had to make sure all the tedious and grinding jobs were completed. He always worked hard and fast to get to the riding out stage of the day. The racetrack was always full of people looking at animals and riders to spot potential winners. Stuart had a superb riding technique and, as often happens in the racing game, good news travels fast within the fraternity, and he was headhunted. He was transferred with Mr Bell's consent to a bigger yard in Newmarket. Someone had obviously spotted him in action and there he was, after only six months, in the trade working for Clive Price. Stuart felt he was destined for the big time. Mr Price had a stable supported by major owners, contained many high-class horses and a top jockey in Willie Carson, also a Scot. His new post was in a different league from any job in Scotland.

Stuart grasped his big chance with both hands; he was on first name terms with household names, famous owners, trainers and jockeys such as Lester Piggott, Joe Mercer and Geoff Lewis to name but a few. He knuckled down to his new job. He behaved impeccably. He was promoted within the yard soon after he had arrived. Mr Price was really impressed by him. He liked how Stuart wanted to learn and improve, and how well he was able to control even the most cantankerous animals. When he was riding out, he displayed good tactical awareness and an ability to follow instructions. His breakthrough came when Mr Price called him into his office from the training track:

"Stuart, I have been watching your progress, I feel you're ready to ride in public. How do you feel?" he asked.

"Confident," he replied, "ready to do what you want."

"Good," he said, "I've been discussing you with Lady Woodcote and we'd like you to ride Red Bonnie at Goodwood on Saturday. You know the horse well. It's a mile handicap and he's been given a low weight. Willie (the top jockey) can't do the weight, so we're relying on you. Can you do it?"

Stuart was thrilled. He had jumped up the pecking order in the stable. He knew the horse very well. He was ready to put years of effort into practise.

"Of course, I can, just try and stop me!"

He phoned home to tell everyone about his big day and his first ride. He called home regularly and would always give his dad tips from headquarters. His dad would cascade the information and, pretty often, the local bookies took a hell of a beating. This time it was different, Stuart had suddenly become a local celebrity. The *Daily Record* included a small article letting people know it was the little Scottish jockey's first public ride.

The big day arrived. The race was televised on *Grandstand*. Everyone in Arden was watching. William King, the local bookie, was trying to lay off some of the bets to minimise any possible loss. Stuart was driven to Goodwood in Suffolk in the trainer's car. Mr Price spent most of the journey discussing race tactics and the opposition with him.

The stable did not expect to win, but wanted Red Bonnie to do well. He was nervous as he left to go and get changed into the owner's colours in the dressing room. He and their other jockeys weighed in and then set out for the paddock. He had to pinch himself to see if he was dreaming or was it really him amongst the rich and famous.

He went out into the paddock where he met the owner, Lady Woodnote, who was with her husband and Mr Price. Mr Price gave Stuart some last-minute advice and a leg up onto Red Bonnie. He relaxed the horse as he trotted down to the starting stalls. The rider was oblivious to the betting frenzy, which was happening on the course and in bookmaker shops across the country. There was a red-hot favourite in the race called Smart Alex, ridden by Eddie Hide, but Stuart's mount was ten to one. The race started at a slow pace which suited Red Bonnie as she had good finishing speed. The novice jockey waded his way through the field and then, with perfect timing, took the lead two furlongs from home. His heart pounded as he kicked for home. He could not hear anything behind him for the roar of the crowd. He won, his first race and he won.

He waved his hand in the air, simultaneously his family and the inhabitants of Arden were going wild with excitement. He guided the horse into the paddock to be greeted warmly by his boss and was the recipient of a large hug from the owner. Life just couldn't getter any better, he imagined – but it did.

Stuart began to get more riding opportunities, he continued to send tips back home. The entire stables' owners were taking an interest in him as his abilities developed. He was becoming even more popular with the stable lassies too. He rode fourteen winners from his first sixty rides in his first season as an apprentice. All was going well, until his old weaknesses began to resurface.

As his rise up the social ladder accelerated, so too did his taste in clothes, food and social activities. He had to have the best clothes to impress the girls, he had to take them to the swankiest places and he had to give no indication of the background he had come from. However, as an eighteen-year-old second-year apprentice, his success was not matched by an increment in wages. Like most apprentices, he still had to rely on the generosity of the owners to make a decent wage.

Stuart's success on the track continued. He was meeting more and more influential people, he called his mum to tell her that he had met 'The Queen Murra'. However, he, as I said, began to drift into his old ways. He just could not resist the opportunity and the ease to escape suspicion. It started in the jockeys' changing room. He would pilfer small but hard to trace, easy to hide objects. He would remove watches, cuff-links, gold chains, riding crops and most of all, wallets. He was sly enough to avoid being caught and, at first, was not a suspect. Items were beginning to go missing, but the jockeys all thought of an outsider – why would it be one of their own? He continued to be popular with the owners because Stuart had no weight problems, regardless of how much he ate or drank. He was losing popularity amongst his peers because there were just one too many coincidences, how was it every time he was around, someone always lost a piece of property or money? A lot of people were beginning to think the common denominator was Stuart – even if no one could ever prove it.

Mr Price began to become concerned; Stuart was one of the more popular lads in the yard. He sensed people were beginning to give him a wide berth. He thought, perhaps, it was jealousy as he had come a long way in a short time, but he had heard the whispers. At first, Mr Price did not confront him since there was no evidence whatsoever to connect him to any crime and, after all, many of the crimes were so petty that none had been officially reported to the police, but many racecourses now decided to install CCTV cameras in restricted areas. Belatedly, he decided he had to act.

One Sunday, in the middle of the horseracing season, Mr Price invited Stuart to lunch to talk over engagements in the forthcoming week and when he would be riding at which meeting. He arrived on time along with a few other lads, who needed to know what preparations had to be made. Mr Price started talking about the riding arrangements for that week, and then he excused himself to go to the bathroom. When he went into the toilet, he took off his gold Rolex and left it on the windowsill above the wash hand basin. He then came back into the room. He finished the meeting quickly as he knew it was the only day off for most of the lads, but he asked Stuart to stay as he wanted to talk to him about a particular horse. All the others left, only Stuart and Mr Price were in the house. They started talking about a horse called Hercules who had classic potential. Eventually, Stuart went to the toilet. As soon as he was there, his beady eyes spotted the watch. His kleptomania overcame him. He had to have it. He came back into the lounge and continued to discuss racing matters with the boss. He did not panic or flinch or behave in any way untoward. Mr Price mulled over his next step. He excused himself again.

He saw his watch had been taken. It could only have been Stuart. He was angry and disappointed. He decided to ask him to return it.

Stuart protested his innocence:

"I don't know what you mean, Mr Price. I didn't touch any watch. Go on search me if you like – you won't find anything on me."

"I daresay I wouldn't, Stuart, but the police might, old chap!" Mr Price said in his superior tone, "C'mon, Stuart, last chance, own up."

Stuart knew the game was up. He hadn't had any time to dispose of the watch. He had been careless in his actions. He tried to play on the price of loyalty. He pledged it would never happen.

He begged for forgiveness. He told him he would make it up to him. He pleaded for compassion and not to be handed over to the police. The renowned trainer, who genuinely really liked Stuart, could not believe that he could have stolen from him after all he had done to enrich his life. Against his better judgement, he told Stuart he would not go to the police. He wanted to dismiss him from the yard and tell him he would never work again, but he felt he had to give him a chance to make amends. He demanded that Stuart should seek treatment for his illness. He realised that this little scoundrel had been responsible for a great deal of the theft which had taken place. He told him he would arrange for him to see a top sports psychologist, and if he did not agree to seek treatment, he was effectively banned from the racing game. Stuart had embraced the sport of kings and was once again a pauper, in the trust of a benefactor.

Stuart immediately agreed to do anything Mr Price asked of him. He loved his new life and would have done anything to preserve it. He knew it was his last chance because, he knew if his penchant for theft leaked out, he would have been finished in the racing world.

The next day, Mr Price sent Stuart to meet Professor O.I. Lovett, a well-known sports psychologist who had treated many top sportsmen and women with a range of problems, addictions and the like. Mr Price was convinced the poor sod was worth the effort and expense. Stuart did have a genuine, rare horse-riding talent

Stuart had met many psychologists in his previous life. He knew the script and this one turned out to be no different from all the others. Stuart participated in all the psychometric assessment tests, and then was interviewed intensively by the acclaimed doctor. He listened intently to all the mumbo-jumbo, all the buzzwords, all the jargon. He went along with his conclusion that he stole because he had a hang-up about his diminutive size, and that this made him behave the way he did. Once again, Stuart was informed he had 'Wee Man's Syndrome'. Stuart stayed the course. He knew within himself that size didn't matter, but he played the game and accepted Professor Lovett's positive pronouncements of the advantages at being small, He emerged from the treatment a better man, having confronted his demons. Mr Price was satisfied that Stuart was cured. Stuart was cured. He vowed never to get caught again.

Stuart then resumed a very successful racing career for the next thirty years. He never reached the upper echelons of the sport, but he carved out a good lifestyle for himself. In thirty years, he rode in eighteen thousand races, he had 2,769 winners, 1,017 second places and 410 thirds. He won over five million pounds for owners and trainers. He also amassed ten thousand and nine hundred and fifty gifts (as he called them). These gifts included sixteen hundred watches, one thousand pairs of cufflinks, eight hundred rings and thousands of sundry pieces of jewellery as well as eight hundred and seventy-five wallets containing sixty thousand pounds at least. Stuart thought of this as cheap at the price. He was never apprehended for any of the crimes. He retired to Australia with his family. He had stolen in four continents, but did not do so in Asia as he was always given superb presents by Arabian owners and, moreover, he did not wish his hands to be cut off. He had indeed come a long way from humble beginnings.

The Makeup Girl

She was born at home in Pollokshaws, Glasgow Southside, on a breezy autumn night. It had been a difficult delivery for her mother. The midwives explained that since it had been over twenty years since her last child was born, her body had become less adept at giving birth. Marina was a late baby. Her parents, Sadie and Bert, had been taken aback by the news of her pregnancy. Their marriage was cold and stale. The new-born had not revitalised it but instead made them more resentful towards each other. This was reflected in the way they parented her. The relationship was detached and miserable, and the poor child constantly felt she was a nuisance who was just in the way. She got that one right.

Her two sisters were twenty-five and twenty-three years older than her. They did not waste any time hanging around Glasgow. They had both married good, solid tradesmen and emigrated to Canada and Australia respectively. Marina knew of their existence but they never came home, even for a holiday, and her parents never went to see them. Communication was restricted to Christmas cards. She longed to see and meet them and possibly stay with them, but that offer never came. She blamed her parents. They were so distant and remote with each other, how they could ever be close to people, even family, thousands of miles away. She had to accept her fate as an unwanted child stuck in a loveless world. She could not say that she was neglected. She was clothed in the best of gear and fed the best of food, but she was starved of love, closeness and affection.

Marina, unlike her parents, was gregarious. She was popular in school. She attracted many friends. She was different. Her dress sense reflected the psychedelic sixties.

She was zany and bohemian much to the annoyance of her parents. She was not academic but she was very colourful and creative. She used to dress her friends' hair and had a penchant for applying makeup. She drove her parents to distraction as a teenager. They were both in their early sixties. She was a teenager. The imaginary revolution of the young had begun. This coincided with Marina's first foray into the labour market. She had landed a dream job working at the No 7 makeup counter within Boots the Chemist. Her vivacious personality and peroxide-blonde hair got her noticed. She was very quickly promoted to senior sales assistant. Her enthusiasm was infectious.

At home, life was humdrum. Parents wishing, without actually saying, that she would meet someone and ride off into the sunset like her elder siblings had done before her. She longed for that to happen too and it was not long before it did. For she was just days shy of her eighteenth birthday when she met Alistair at the Plaza ballroom. It was not one of her usual haunts. She preferred live music places like the Alpen Lodge or the Dennistoun Palais. This was a disco. The lights were low, the noise unbearably loud as he sallied over to ask her to dance. She liked the look of him. He was tall, confident, a cut above the average looking and available. They had a few dances and a short conversation which led to telephone numbers being exchanged. She had no intention of phoning him, she was not prudish but she just wouldn't have made that kind of first move, she did hope he would call her.

The next day, the call she had been waiting for came. Alistair wanted to see her again. The first few weeks were a bliss. He wined and dined her at the top spots. She became a very familiar face in the Rogano and the Royal Automobile Club to name but a few. He showered her with expensive gifts and sent flowers with romantic messages to her workplace. She was quickly falling for him. The affair soon started in earnest. She resisted his physical advances until the sixth date, and then she finally submitted in his car on the quiet road to Ayr. Alistair was an experienced lover. He knew his way around a woman's body. He usually took precautions on every occasion, but on the first occasion he was so carried away with excitement that he was rather careless. That initial mistake led to an unplanned pregnancy which had transforming effects on both their lives.

Alistair wanted to do the right thing by Marina. He proposed that they marry. She was madly in love and accepted without delay. They secretly planned their wedding. Marina decided she would not tell her parents. She simply left them a note stating that she had eloped with Alistair, a man they had never met. She said she would be in touch in time and advised them not to worry. Alistair came from a well-off background. His parents set them up in a one-bedroom flat in Shawlands. She was blissfully happy.

The couple settled well early on the marriage. She continued to work in Boots. His dad had given him a pay hike to reflect his new status. The first time she noticed anything strange about Alistair was when he started quizzing her about her work, who she had spoken to that day and about her male boss. He had never done so before, so she was a little taken aback. Then he began to criticise her housekeeping skills – especially her cooking skills. Marina began to get frustrated with his constant nagging and his expectations that she should be available to him at all times. She controlled her emotions. She was, after all, expecting a new arrival within a few months and thought she was just adjusting to married life. A crisis point came when Alistair told her she should not return to work after the baby was born – he wanted her to be a full-time mum. Marina had no intention of giving up the job she loved but he laboured the point and forced her hand. He went so far as to contact her manager to insist that she be told that she could not return due to company policy on employing married women. He began to overstep the mark regularly and dismiss any challenge she made to his opinions. Marina was in a quandary. She decided she would write to her parents to let them know where she was and what was happening in her life. She thought they might have responded to her letter but they never did.

She gave birth to Martin right on her due date in St Francis of Assisi private hospital. Both mother and baby were fit and healthy. Alistair and his parents were ecstatic. It was the first new-born in their family for some considerable time. When they arrived back home, everything for the baby was new, pristine and the most expensive of all brands available. Alistair spared no expense, however, as the weeks progressed, he became more controlling and demanding with her. He wanted her to account for her every movement for each day, he criticised her maternal skills, accused her of neglect, putting on too much makeup, not attending to his needs and desires and preferring other people's company. Marina grew tired of his incessant complaints, but the final straw came when he lifted his hand to her because she had not given him tea in the proper cup. She wanted to leave as this first initial slap he had got away with, opened the floodgates as he began to hit her with increasing regularity and severity. She told no one. She had no one to tell. She was isolated and felt that no one would believe that a respectable man like Alistair would be capable of such acts.

One day, he set off for work, ignoring her as usual, she decided to escape with baby Martin, who was now nine months old. She had to return to her parents' home. There was nowhere else to go. Her parents were unwelcoming but agreed that she could stay until she got her life sorted out, the proviso was that they did not want their lives disrupted. They would under no circumstances babysit; whenever she went out, the baby went with her and she would take the baby to and from the nursery every day. All the days were the same, work, baby, work and home. Every night, her dad went to the pub, her mother went to bingo. Even if she went to the shops for a paper, she had to take Martin with her. She thought they thought she would do a runner if she was let out. This routine carried on for weeks. Alistair bombarded her with phone calls. He waited for her outside her work. He pleaded with her to come back. He promised it would all be different. He accepted full blame for his actions. He promised her and the baby a new, better life. Marina felt like she was between the devil and the deep blue sea. She had hoped her parents would have softened and maybe even taken to the one grandchild they could physically see – but they never did. They had no heart. She decided she would give Alistair another chance. They would make a new start. Alistair parents helped him to buy a three-bedroom house in Thornwood, a cosy residential area.

The first few years of their new start were lovely. Alistair was a model husband. They had two more children, both girls, Amy and Amanda. Alistair expanded his father's business. Marina gone back to Boots on a very part-time basis as agreed. They had no financial worries; the kids were growing up and had started school. Suddenly, Alistair began to go back to his old ways. He started to criticise everything she did, her dress sense, the way she dealt with the kids, her job, her lack of academic ability and her social skills. This went on for a year, then he began to turn his attention to Martin. Martin was an indoor boy, he preferred to build things, read books, play board games and watch television. He was a well-behaved boy but Alistair just couldn't leave him alone. He challenged him constantly. He began to use physical violence when the boy answered back. He behaved differently towards him and his sisters. Alistair resented the wee boy and it showed. He used to rant at him:

"Why can't you go out and play football with the other boys, you little poof!"

Marina watched her son's confidence being taken from him remorselessly until she could stand it no more. Not only was she being abused, she could take that for the sake of the kids, but she could not stand to see her boy being demoralised for absolutely no reason. She began to despise her husband.

She belatedly decided to act. She sought legal advice promptly. She was advised to divorce Alistair and given proper support to claim all she was entitled to. Alistair was very submissive about her actions. He simply acceded to all her lawyers' requests and gave her half of his estate with which she bought her house. Marina was surprised at the ease she was able to release herself and her children from the marriage. He agreed to her terms and conditions on access, maintenance and basically left her to it. Why had he done so? Perhaps, he was as unhappy as she was or, maybe he already had a replacement lined up. She didn't really care. All she wanted to do was to protect herself and her children from the physical and psychological abuse she had endured for too long. She knew it would be difficult on her own with three kids but she relished the challenge. Her main aim was to get Martin recovered from his ordeal. She knew how badly he was affected as on the first day in their new house, he told her:

"Thanks, Mum, for taking me away from that evil monster."

Marina wasn't under any illusions concerning how difficult life was going to be on her own, but she still retained that fighting determination to succeed. She ground out the next few years. The girls were very like her in nature – flamboyant, exuberant and somewhat bohemian; Martin was an introvert. She handled him delicately and sensitively. She continued to progress in work at No 7 counter. Amy and Amanda went to Art and Design College. They graduated and both found work as floor and window designers with Primark and House of Fraser. Both were then promoted and transferred to America for their firms. Martin continued to be a problem and stayed at home. He worked as a civil servant but did not have a huge social circle. He did eventually meet a partner who turned out to be the making of him. Marina was delighted that, at last, Martin had found a soulmate – it took the pressure off her and freed her to crack on with her own life.

She began to start going out again. By now, she was in her fifties and found it difficult to meet other people. She would have liked to have had another relationship, but all she mustered were a few internet-dating disasters. She was looking for Mr Right, but all she seemed to meet was Mr Right-Now. She did, however, have one interesting night in the Scotia Bar, an old haunt of hers. She was on a night out with some friends from Boots. She sat next to a woman around the same age as herself. The woman looked forlorn and upset. Elizabeth, naturally concerned, asked her if she was all right.

"Why the long face?" she enquired, "Can't be that bad."

"I just lost my husband three months ago, and it would have been his birthday tomorrow. Never even got to 55."

"What happened to him?" Elizabeth enquired sympathetically

"Alistair had cancer. Spread like wildfire – everywhere within two months."

After a couple more exchanges, it turned out that Marina and the woman had been married to the same man. Marina had long since lost any contact with him. She was inwardly glad that he had got his comeuppance.

"Tell me this, Mavis, did he do to you what he did to me?"

"Once or twice, but it was always my fault. He was a good man."

"Aye, right!" she said before moving away.

Marina just carries on with her life in No 7 Boots counter at Silverburn. At 67, she has no plans to retire. She is still trying to meet someone – maybe, an elderly gent. She is still glamorous and energetic. Her life will be lonely, at least until her two girls come back from the States. Her main challenge now is trying to make septuagenarian Glaswegian housewives to look like Lady Gaga.

Her remote control has become her best friend, but she is always optimistic that things can only get better.

The Party

Steven was 40 that day but he had not planned any celebrations as he and Elizabeth were getting married the very next week. It seemed a bit too expensive to have two parties. He thought why not kill two birds with one stone. Elizabeth, on the other hand, felt a bit sorry for him, not really doing anything to acknowledge an important milestone in his life. So, she started to arrange a small surprise in their flat with just a few family and friends.

Elizabeth booked a table for her and Steven at the Wok Way, their favourite restaurant, for seven o'clock on Saturday evening. She fixed it for her sister, Lynn, to invite all the guests and prepare all the food which would be brought to the house, whilst she and Steven were out having their meal. I was there just as a friend from work. There was only one other person I knew. The rest of the party was made up of both their parents, one granny, their respective sisters and brothers and a few selected very long-term friends. There were about 15 people there in total.

We were all sitting there in a huddle. There was an especially relaxed atmosphere as Lynn laid out the food in the kitchen and served everyone with a welcoming drink. The conversation was communal and cordial as we all awaited the arrival of the main man. Lynn explained they were at a restaurant not far away and that Elizabeth would text her to let us know when they were on their way. The idea was to turn out all the lights and surprise him on arrival.

"Can't believe that my Steven turned forty!" declared Mary, his mum. "Oh my God, he has been some boy, hasn't he, Jimmy?"

"You can say that again – trouble right from the start," he said jokingly. "Mary, tell them about Ibrox."

We all listened intently, especially me, as she shared her memories. Couldn't wait to hear more about Steven for banter value in work.

"Oh God!" she sighed, "His very first game as a ball boy at Ibrox, big John Greig belted a pile driver bang onto Steven's nose. Out cold he was. Skelped him right in the kisser. Stretchered off in the first minute. He made the paper getting presented with the match ball. Still got the ball and the picture."

"Aye, an' he's still got the bent nose," quipped Jimmy

"This is Steven for you," said Jimmy, as if no one would believe what he was going to tell you. "See, our very first holiday abroad. We went to Sidari in Corfu. We were in an apartment with no pool so we had to go to the beach for sunbathing. It was very hot. The beaches were quite shingly near the flat. We decided to go further afield to get to the sandiest beach. We trekked for 40 minutes, carrying all the towels, lotions, potions, lunch, and drinks. I was knackered. Got to the beach. Unpacked and laid out all the gear for the day. Lay down on the lounger. Not even two minutes later, all we heard was a loud '*AAAAARGH*'. Just knew who it would be. Steven bitten by a jellyfish. We had to quickly pack up, try to find a local chemist carrying him on my shoulder. What a jolly holiday that was!"

"Still doesn't swim in the sea," Jimmy added.

"Oh, Mum," Karen, his sister, giggled, "tell them about the time Steven burnt his arse in the toilet."

"In fairness," said Mary in all seriousness, "that wasn't his fault. I had actually poured paraffin down the toilet pan instead of bleach by mistake. Then, the bold Steven, he was only about 13 or 14 at the time, decided he would have a fly teenage smoke in the bathroom. In he goes, sits on the pan, strikes a match to light the fag and throws the flaming match onto the paraffin in the bowl. Oh my God! I have never heard such a shriek in all my life as Steven ran out of the toilet, backside on fire. Jimmy threw water on him and we took him to A&E again!"

"Still doesn't smoke," quipped Jimmy

Lynn got a text at around 8:30, it said, *"FFS, going to be delayed, big barney in the kitchen. Waited 30 mins for starter."*

"PMSL, don't panic, we're just blethering here. Getting pissed."

Karen said, "The most I can remember about Steven when I was a wee girl was how he used to practice the moonwalk, and he used to go to work on a Friday dressed as Adam Ant."

"My God!" his granny, Freda, piped up, "What would have his boss thought of him. Where is he anyway? I'm missing strictly."

"There's been a delay in the restaurant, Freda, they'll be here soon."

Lynn said that she thought everybody must have a Steven and Elizabeth story. She was dead right. Her dad, Tommy, he recalled the night when they got locked out of their car in Pollok Park in the dead of night in the pouring rain and how when they arrived home drenched. He remembered them trying to explain away that how and why they had both got out of the front of the car top to get into the back of the car. They tried their best but we all knew what they were up to.

Another text message, *"That's us leaving the restaurant. C u in ten."*

"Right, they'll be here soon. Charge your glasses and we'll put the lights out!" Lynn stated.

We were all sitting in the dark. We saw their car stopping outside the close. They both got out of the car. They seemed to be having some sort of altercation (not quite a rammy). They didn't come up the stairs, instead headed round the corner to the pub.

Another text message, *"FFS, can't get him up the stairs. Says it's only nine."*

Lynn replied, *"Hurry up, Granny's rantin'. Use ur feminine wiles."*

We all waited patiently in the dark.

"Wonder why they decided to wed now. Bit of a hurry after all this time together. Is she pregnant?" Freda thought out loud.

"Don't be daft, Gran."

Elizabeth urged Steven just to have one drink. She whispered sweet nothings to him. She told him she was really going to make his birthday special when they were in the house. Steven quickly finished his drink. Elizabeth asked the barmaid to keep all his birthday drinks on tap. They said their cheerios and meandered towards home.

We all looked out of the bay window. We could see Steven with his arm wrapped round Elizabeth. They were kissing passionately in the street. We heard the close door opening. They took their time coming up to their landing. Steven unbuckled his belt in hasty anticipation of what was to come. The front door sprung open and there was Steven, his trousers had fallen down to his ankles.

Surprise! Surprise! It most certainly was. I found out more about Steven in those two hours than I had in the twenty years I'd known him for. Sweet memories.

A Granny Story

Once upon a time in a tiny, wee village called Thornliebank, Lisa and Martin were sitting watching *iCarly* on Nickelodeon via Sky, since Lisa had won the television fight that day, when their mum came in to the living room and made a surprise announcement.

"Right, kids, get ready to go down to your gran's house. Your dad and I are having a night out and Granny has agreed to look after you two for us!"

"Oh, no, Mum, do we have to? What about dinner? Why can't you just pick us up after your night out? You know we both hate staying there!" the kids almost said in unison.

"There's no debate about it. Your granny is making your dinner and we'll see you both in the morning. Now, not another word." she replied firmly.

After Dad had returned from work and got himself cleaned up to go out, they set off in the car. Not a word spoken but the atmosphere was tense, as if both kids felt they were about to enter a warzone rather than enjoy an overnight stay with a cuddly pensioner. The family emerged from the car to be greeted with a warm smile from a loving Gran. The adults exchanged pleasantries, the kids were duly warned to behave themselves and the deal was made for them to be picked up no later than ten o'clock the next morning. Mum and Dad left Lisa and Martin in the care of their ever-loving, but very old-fashioned gran.

Lisa looked at her granny and wondered if she had ever been without her tattered old cardigan and her worn out slippers. If she had, she had never seen her. She made up her mind that when she grew up, she was going to take charge of her gran's wardrobe and force her into this millennium –

whether she liked it or not. Lisa questioned why none of her aunts or uncles ever said anything to Gran about the way she was. Martin just accepted Granny the way she was and thought all grannies must be the same since he met his friend Peter's gran, she too had a torn cardigan and smelled of age.

"Right!" said Gran, "I better get you both fed. I've made a big pot of mince n' tatties for you. Lisa, go and turn that television off, I don't allow television at mealtimes. Martin, go and sit down at the table."

The two children looked as though they had been struck down by a thunderbolt, no telly at teatime, sitting down together and MINCE? What was the world coming to? How could their parents be so cruel as to leave them in this so nutritious environment?

Martin was shocked but hungry, so he did not raise any objections and just ate the tasty food, but Lisa dared to speak out.

"Granny, I don't like mince, can I have something else?" she muttered apprehensively.

"What? What do you mean you don't like my mince? Do you think you're in a fancy restaurant, ya cheeky wee midden? If you're hungry enough, you'll eat it! And I'll tell you what – if you don't eat it tonight, you'll get it tomorrow for breakfast! Honestly! I've never heard the like," the indignant woman ranted.

"Sorry, I am just not hungry for mince at the moment, Gran," squirmed Lisa.

The ambiance in Granny's house simmered as they all moved on from the teatime spat. It was going to be a long night if it carried on in this vein. Martin, as always, interrupted the silence.

"Granny, can I watch *Kerching*? It's on Channel 670 on Sky."

"My telly only goes up to Channel 5! I don't have Sky. Why the hell do you need all those channels anyway? You'll just have to content yourself with what I got – and be grateful for it," smarted Gran. They watched *CBeebies* instead.

Martin's eyes rolled to the roof, Lisa was frustrated and hungry but didn't want to offend her granny again – so she said nothing and tried to think about what she could do to update her granny. *This granny needs a transformation*, she kept thinking.

Martin piped up again as if he was quite oblivious to his grandmother's mood.

"Granny, I've brought my Xbox down with me, can I plug it in to the back of your television and give you a game?"

"What's an Xbox, I thought it was a SP2 you had? Will it mess up my television?"

"It was a PS2 and I have moved on to Xbox – it's even better. And no, it won't mess up your telly – I do it all the time at home."

So, Martin attached his SCAT plug to the television and gave Granny an interesting demonstration on how to twiddle the knobs, press the buttons and move the controls. His granny was amazed at all the skills this small boy possessed. Not only could he do it, but he was also able to explain to her in her own tongue so that she could understand what she was doing.

After this, Granny just left Martin to his own devices. She never really watched her television at night, preferring to read or knit. While Martin was engrossing himself on his Xbox, Lisa helped her gran to clear up the dishes. In the course of the conversation, Lisa was telling her elder about the capabilities of her mobile phone. She showed her granny how she could take a photo or make a video recording, and then send it all over the world just through her phone. Granny was amazed and shocked and thrilled by the technology. If she hadn't seen with her own eyes, she wouldn't have believed all this was possible. Mary blethered away with her gran all night. Granny was exhausted as she probed her about how she lived since she had been left on her own. Granny was taken aback by how mature these two kids were, and so enamoured that they were both taking such an interest in her as a person. She was moved and decided from that moment on that she had to move on with her life, instead of just vegetating. As the evening wore on, she became very tired. She was an involuntary victim of information overload. And so, she ordered the two kids to bed, where Lisa scoffed two cakes she had hidden in her bag.

The next morning, Gran woke the two children up at seven o'clock. She organised them as if they were in the army, and soon they were washed, groomed and sparkling – ready for the day. She sat them quietly in her sitting room and forbade them from ogling at the television. It was an absolutely unbreakable custom.

"Right! You two come through here. Martin, here's your ham n' eggs – eat them up. Lisa, here's yours," she said straight-facedly.

Mary was presented with the mince and potatoes she had refused to eat the night before. Her face said it all as she used her puppy dog eyes to remonstrate with her gran.

"Gran, mince for breakfast! Are you having a laugh?"

Granny Hill was aghast at her granddaughter's blind insolence, she realised that the girl didn't even realise she was being cheeky. Her face creased into a wizened grin and she, for the first time in her life, gave in to a child. She couldn't think what had come over her, why had she mellowed overnight. She gave Lisa the food she had prepared for herself and made some more toast for herself which she shared with the kids. She really didn't want their parents to return, but they did as they had been told and arrived at ten o'clock to retrieve their babies. Their departure was, for some unknown reason, more emotional and tender than it had ever been before and they promised to phone her soon.

A few days later, a strange thing happened. Granny Hill phoned her daughter for a change and asked her for Lisa and Martin's email address.

"What do you want to know that for, Mum? Are you feeling all right? Do you want me to come over?"

"I've never been better!" she glowed, "I just want to surprise them. Now, don't say anything to them about this!"

Later that evening as the family were sitting down for their evening meal, in front of the television as usual, their computer beeped, '*You have email*'.

Martin went over to the computer to check for messages,

"Wow! I don't believe it. Lisa, come and see this! It looks like we've got an email from Granny asking us to come. No way, how would Granny ever be able to send us a message!" Martin shrieked.

The four of them starred at the screen in disbelief. How was this possible for someone who still had a steam kettle and a hat with a brooch in it?

They rushed into the car and made their way over to Granny's house to see if she was OK. She opened the door, her old cardigan had gone to be replaced by a bright, pink T-shirt which had 'CHEEKY' emblazoned in shiny letters across her chest. Her crimplene trousers were now blue denims. They stepped back in amazement as she welcomed them into her house.

"Martin, I'm dying to show you my new Xbox. Promise me you will show me how to work it. All the games are two players – so you need to help me," Granny she gushed.

"Lisa, would you program my new Freeview Box. I might get Sky later. Stand there till I take a picture of you with my new mobile," she said as though it was no big deal.

Lisa, Martin and their mum and dad were for once stunned into temporary silence. They just didn't know what to do or say. Martin, as usual, recovered first.

"Granny, what games did you get?"

"I bought *FIFA 15* for you and *The Simpsons* to play with Lisa – now I hope you will help me to get plenty of practice in. My internet connection came today."

"No bother, Granny, you are just the tops," Martin quipped

"Right, Gran, that's your telly sorted, look you'll be able to watch loads of channels now. You'll like *Challenge* if you like quiz shows. C'mon, I will show you how to text me, in case you get stuck."

But you know what, Granny never got stuck for fun or company again as she revelled in the love of her two fantastic grandchildren and joined the local community centre to learn how to use technology. Her now motto was 'Change is good – embrace it'.

Well-Hidden Talent

According to a very well-known song, some guys have all the luck, some guys have all the pain, Garry definitely fell into the former category. He wasn't quite born with silver spoon syndrome, but he came from an upper working-class family, if such an entity exists. Both his parents had good jobs. His dad was an engineer and his mum was a school secretary. They lived in a newly built council estate just created in the early 1950s, as Britain was trying to reconstruct it's infrastructure after the Second World War.

The couple, in modern terms, would be described as upwardly mobile compared to most folks who lived in their street. It was a far cry from his upbringing in the cold, harsh Orcadian landscape of the twenties, where some of his family still lived in the farm breeding beef cattle for a living. Life was tough for Garry's father. His grandparents eked out a living on the farm which the family ran for years and years. His grandfather finally gave up his share of the land to his brother who had no such notion to leave the island despite the bleak, cold climate. The family moved to Glasgow to enrich their lives and find an income which could sustain, and to an extent had succeeded in this aim. Garry's dad, Murdo, had received a better education than he would have, he progressed through an apprenticeship and had been fortunate enough to meet the love of his life, Kate, just two doors down from the tenement where his brood settled.

Murdo and Kate married after a short romance – they were both getting on a bit at 25. They first moved into a room and kitchen in Mount Florida in the south side of Glasgow. They saved and saved, hoping that their application for one of the new houses wouldn't take too long. Their aspirations were met and they were allocated a brand-new house in Woodfarm, not far from their places of work.

They were happy and content. Their life became complete when Kate discovered that she was expecting their first child, soon after they had accepted the tenancy for their new property. Life was fine and dandy until a paediatric error caused a lack of oxygen to reach the newborn baby's brain, resulting in the child being left with learning difficulties. The couple coped well with their boy's condition. Callum was a very much wanted and loved addition to their family. He was well looked after and they sought advice and support (little as there was at that time) from the medical authorities. They tried to raise him with as normal a life as they could. Callum's condition did not deter them from adding to their family, and four years later, Garry was born. Another four years passed and they were gifted with a sister Janice. As you can imagine, all of their lives' were affected by the special treatment and attention Callum needed, but Murdo and Kate were devoted to their family and provided the best for every one of them.

As time moved on, Murdo and Kate were presented with more problems arising from Callum's behaviour. He was not coping with mainstream school, other families were cruel and complained their kids' were frightened by Callum. Callum himself was oblivious to the issues he was causing. He was just a noisy boisterous adolescent who was a bit slow to pick up lessons. To cut a long story short, after plenty of resistance and battling with the authorities, Callum, as were many others in his situation, was committed to Lennox Castle Hospital which looked after people who had mental health issues. The facility was completely inappropriate and heart breaking for his parents, but they could do nothing to prevent his incarceration. It was not until many years later, long after Murdo and Kate had died, that it was established that many people who were institutionalised in these hospitals were better off being supported in their community. Some 40 years later, Callum was released and placed in supported accommodation. Sad.

The main effect of Callum being forced to live away from his home and family was that that Garry and Janice were able to live more normal lives away from the cruel taunts they had to endure yet not understand as they were growing up. Their parents were able to spend more time with them and to an extent, compensate for their hardships by lavishing them with luxuries that most kids in their location would not have access to. The family were fairly affluent, they were able to take the kids abroad on holiday in the early 60s, they had a car and were considered to be better off than their peers. The kids themselves were developing normally. Garry was a clever, semi-handsome boy who seemed to go through school getting great marks effortlessly. His sister seemed to take longer to recover from the traumas the family suffered at the hands of a few ignorant people who never let them forget they had a brother in Lennox Castle. Kids can be very cruel.

***

The two siblings developed into typical teenagers. The boy seemed to just go with the flow, insignificant, wimpy, part of the crowd, not particularly noticeable or sporty or talented. The girl, throughout her adolescent years, became feistier and more temperamental. She started to avoid school, began to indulge in drugs and alcohol at a younger age than most, and mixed with the wrongdoers. Their parents' continued to support them and did their utmost to help. Through their teens, they still visited their eldest boy weekly. The kids, like all teenagers do, lost interest in hospital visits – more concerned with their own activities and friends. Who knows why they stopped going to see Callum. Maybe their parents didn't force them, maybe it was the stench of the hospital, could have been the zombification of their brother, the sight of patients having seizures and fits during the visits, the knowledge that all of their brother's possessions were missing and the staff were disinterested in their complaints or maybe they just didn't care enough?

It was just shortly after this period, just as he entered sixth form, the transformation started. All of a sudden from nowhere, girls started to take an inordinate interest in Garry. His friends were very envious and wanted to know the secret of how he could, without any effort, attract any chick in the year. Countless times at school social occasions, his friends spent hours preparing to dress well, smell nice and use the right lines to chat up the girls. Garry didn't. He just strolled on to the dancefloor and before you could say Burt Reynolds, there he was in a passionate clench with some girl he hadn't even spoken to. What was his magic trick? His friends had spent hours practicing their chat-up techniques without effect. There was this seemingly skinny, blue-eyed, boring, uncharismatic, average looking, spotty youth effortlessly grabbing all the action. He was the boy who matured way more quickly than the rest of them. He had experienced things with the opposite sex they could not imagine. He would attract wide-eyed, large groups as he regaled them with stories of his salacious exploits. The things was that nobody could comprehend why it was him and not them. He was the first in the group to smoke, then quit, while hooking everyone else, he was the first to get a ticket for an Alice Cooper concert at the Apollo, he was the first to bring scud mags into the prefect's room, amongst other firsts, the first to own a college jumper and to get drunk – then stop drinking.

Tension and jealously was palpable in the prefect's room as a pattern emerged from Garry's romantic escapades. He was working his way through the whole year starting from A-Annabelle to Z-Zara. Each affair lasted about a fortnight to three weeks. He dumped them all sans explanation and moved on to the next conquest. He managed to leave the lovers broken hearted and vulnerable – which assisted his friends who became experts at picking up the pieces. He tormented his pals with stories about the affairs. He explained to them that once the chase was over, so was the excitement. He felt no emotion or regret or loss at any of the relationships or the effect they had on his victims. He did not see them as victims but consenting adults. Everything seemed so easy for him compared to his peers; he even seemed to pass his exams without trying too hard. He passed his driving test first time and quite clearly, and was the first to go through intimate teenage rites of passage without suffering the pains. Perhaps it was his generosity that won them over. He had more money and more stuff than anyone else, but he was not mean and often shared his wares with his friends.

Garry carried on in the same vein at university. He didn't seem to have to try but the lady students seem magnetised to him. By the time he had passed his degree, he had slept with the biggest percentage of the girls on the course. Same as school, two to three-week affair, dismiss them by moving onto the next one and ignore the emotional trauma he was contributing to. His success rate was astonishing as he was so ordinary and unexciting and cold. He passed his degree with the minimum of effort – just like school – no drama, no stress, and no problem.

He, then, started his professional career in a huge government department. The office was large and open, full of young professionals. By this time, he was in his late twenties. His behaviour hadn't changed – still a player but he was beginning to feel quite isolated. He was becoming a professional wedding guest as his friends all seemed to be getting matched to partners. For the first time ever, he felt he was missing out. He had countless, meaningless affairs. He couldn't remember half their names. He began to think the FFF rules were getting past their sell-by date. He started to think about settling down but he had to find a suitable and willing partner.

It wasn't long after that Viv joined his department. She was new, late twenties, unmarried and no baggage, seemed like fun and, moreover, didn't know his reputation. The only problem he could see was that she was a high-flier, at least two grades higher than him, would she be interested! He asked her out to dinner is his usual inoffensive manner and found to his delight that she was fun and interesting, but a bit quaint in her ideas. She was a posh girl from the country and laid her cards on the table straightaway as to what her moral values were – very different from his. Whatever their dissimilarities, it worked. It was a whirlwind romance. Within three months, they were engaged. Another six, and they were wed. Garry's friends, as you can imagine, were sceptical about the whole affair.

"He could never commit to one person!"

"Someone should tell the poor woman!"

"It'll never last."

These were the type of comments and reaction he received from his friends, however, he felt he could love her and was desperate to settle down like everyone else. Viv was also so keen to marry and so confident that she could make the marriage work. It was true romance at last. Viv, of all the women he met, had kept him waiting for the physical side of the relationship until the invitations were out. That was the longest six months of this adult life but he knew in his heart that it was worth the wait. He was glad to marry.

The first year was great – new house in the suburbs, love, happiness and fun for both of them. Viv became pregnant after a few months. Both were delighted – it was what they both wanted. They spent their time preparing for the new arrival. The only fly in the ointment was Viv's attitude to lovemaking. She decided it was not healthy for her or the baby once the pregnancy was confirmed. Garry went along with this but felt frustrated and resentful, but he accepted and respected his wife's choice. The baby boy duly arrived and all was well. Viv was on long-term maternity leave and Garry was a proud dad. A perfect picture postcard family.

The following year, Viv returned to work but not long after, and somewhat unexpectedly, became pregnant again. Viv was quite upset but philosophically looked forward to her second baby in three years. She was a mature mum after all. Garry was also surprised but delighted that they would be adding to their family – not so pleased about the physical barriers Viv was imposing on him. Despite his pleas, Viv was adamant that shop was closed temporarily. Soon, she was back on maternity leave again – just before Christmas.

The next episode showed Garry reverting to type. He was at the office Christmas party when Dolina approached him. Serendipity played a conscious part in the angst-ridden love life he had to follow, never more so when he met Dolina. They were an accident waiting to happen. They chatted – small talk. Dolina, who was slightly tipsy, asked him to dance. The evening wore on. Dolina was getting inebriated. He offered her a lift home. They both knew where this was going. He was a sex-starved, full-bloodied male looking for a friend with benefits; she was a lonely, ignored woman, looking for a little bit of attention. Lust took over as the one-off event transformed into a full-blown affair from the New Year. Dolina was complicated. She had three kids, a manic-depressive, debt-ridden husband, and a major drink problem and was desperately lonely. He thought about ending the affair as soon as he possibly could, but he couldn't leave her alone. She was passionate and adventurous. He knew it was wrong, his wife was about to have their second child, but he just couldn't stop himself. Dolina pushed and pushed and pressurised him into making a choice. She wanted to end her marriage and she wanted him to end his. He was torn apart emotionally. He had never experienced real emotion before, save the birth of his first child.

He was called home early that day. Viv had gone into labour. 24th January 1988, his baby daughter arrived. He went home after visiting Viv. She was physically exhausted; he was mentally exhausted. Dolina called his house and confronted him. If he didn't tell her, she would. She wanted a decision and it had to be today – her or Viv? Whatever way, he was going to be found out anyway. He cuddled Simon, his baby boy, and sobbed uncontrollably. He packed his bag and went to the hospital to deliver his news to his unsuspecting wife.

"Vivien, when you come back to the house tomorrow, I won't be there! I'm leaving."

"What do you mean, you won't be there. I need you. My mum can't look after Simon tomorrow. She has to go home to her own house to look after Dad."

"No, Viv, I'm sorry I am leaving for good. I've met someone else and I think it's for the best. Please forgive me, can you forgive me?" he said apologetically.

Viv just cried and cried and sobbed and wept for days. He went home to Dolina, who had split up with her husband the week before. Dolina's husband cracked up under the strain and is still a missing person to this day. Garry never saw his children again as Viv refused him access which he did not contest, such were his feelings of guilt. Happy days.

The next few months were horrible. Her children, young as they were, struggled to cope without their dad and the worry that he had seemingly disappeared from this earth. Viv, naturally, did what scorned women do – she made life as uncomfortable and financially painful as she could. Garry and Dolina, the toxic couple, carried on trying to normalise life and get her children to accept their new lot. They persevered, and eventually, what life they had created, did become normal. The transition came when after a few years they had a child of their own.

Life was never easy. As the years rolled by, Dolina's children developed into rebellious teenagers, never letting their mum forget it was all her fault. Garry adopted his new partner's lifestyle and changed from behind an almost teetotaller to an everyday drinker. As time moved on, their relationship to alcohol was closer than their relationship to each other. They were functioning alcoholics. They managed to hold down professional jobs in the civil service and raise their family. Getting through the tough years, they accumulated large amounts of debt as they continuously lived well beyond their means as they pandered to the demands of their children. Their relationship naturally suffered through their addiction to alcohol and credit cards. Their bodies more debauched and wrinkly, as they aged prematurely – glamourous they were not! Garry latterly suffered so badly, he lost his job through ill health but luckily managed to secure a good severance package to clear their money problems. He entered into rehab to try to overcome his battle with booze – he made several unsuccessful attempts. Dolina didn't try, she was a happy drunk. After 25 years, the couple finally separated. He had to move out as it was her house they lived in. He was on his own for the first time ever.

He moved into rented accommodation, not far from where he used to live. He and Dolina tried to remain on good terms, although it was evident that they could no longer live together. Their daughter was the glue who kept them in touch. One day, completely out of the blue, Garry received a letter from a solicitor's office asking him to contact them in relation to a will where he had been left an inheritance. It turned out a great uncle, his grandfather's brother, had left him a farm in Orkney. Garry was stunned by this news. He contemplated and procrastinated for days as to what he should do with it. Sell it, maybe?

Then one morning, he woke up in a drunken haze.

Fuck it, he thought, *I'm getting out of here. I have pissed off so many people. I need to try to turn my life around. I am going out the way for good*. He decided to move straightaway. There was no point in waiting. What for – nobody needed or wanted him. He made arrangements to evacuate his flat and travelled on the ferry to Orkney. He went to see his new home. He thought a complete change would do him good as he reflected on a life spoilt by wrong choices.

It was a bleak, windy Orcadian day when he moved in to the picturesque cottage on a farmstead about five miles away from Lerwick. He had inherited a small beef cattle herd which were looked after by a local man and his wife, who had worked for his uncle for years. They lived in a cottage about a quarter of a mile away from his house. There was a barn which housed the animals near the cottage. The first day there, Garry invited the couple over to the house to familiarise himself with how things worked on a farm and to get to know them. The couple left after a convivial evening where they were plied with drink, as their host was celebrating his last chance to get away from all his woes. However, during the night, tragedy struck. Garry had gone to this bed, drunk as usual, but he was awoken when he heard strange noises coming from the byre and went to investigate. Using his torchlight, he could see the animals were restless and seemed agitated. He didn't know what to do or why it was so. He thought maybe they were hungry. So, he grabbed a bag of what he thought was cattle feed. He climbed onto the gate of the pen where the bull was located. Unfortunately for him, in his stupor, he fell over the barrier and into the pen. The bull panicked and started to trample the drunk man and gored him to death. He was discovered the next day by the farmhands who had warned him not to go near the angry bull, who was called Karma, as it was temperamental and he had no experience of looking after livestock. To his peril, he ignored their advice. Karma accounted for Garry. His reputation as an Adonis totally debunked.

***

Janice's story is a lot briefer than Garry's. She never fully recovered from the bullying and harassment she received from a very young age. Her parents tried everything they could to help her. Her self-esteem was always ranked low, she continued her demise as a stereotypical unhappy teenager. She seemed to naturally progress into the mire. Firstly, by not going to school, mixing with other troubled and vulnerable kids. She then started to isolate herself, deteriorating into self-harm. She dabbled in some serious drug taking. The final straw came when her parents passed away somewhat prematurely. Her support system evaporated with them. She died of an overdose some three months later. She left no note, she had no hope, no life and no education, childless and blind to the love that was all around her. She was 28.

***

What of Callum? Well! He was one of the last patients to leave Lennox Castle, ironically on 1st April 2002. He had lived there since the early 70s, so he needed to be completely rehabilitated into living independently in the community. He was very fortunate to be allocated to a very conscientious social worker called Stefan. He appreciated and anticipated all the issues Callum would have to deal with as he had a brother of his own with whom he was very involved in the care of, alongside his family.

Stefan secured supported accommodation for Callum in Glasgow Southside. He was instrumental in arranging support for Callum to learn basic life skills like cooking, hygiene; both personal and domestic, and took a personal interest in his welfare way beyond the call of duty. For Callum, his siblings were a distant memory and Stefan became his appointee and had power of attorney. He was able to help Callum make the big decisions in his life.

At the early stages on his integration, there were, as expected, loads of problems mainly around budgeting and Callum's preponderance for listening to 70s pop music at a very loud decibel level. Callum gained his first ASBO for noise not long after his arrival. He drove his neighbours crazy just playing *Get It On* by T-Rex for hours on end. Stefan overcame the noise issue by purchasing earphones, much to everyone's delight. He resolved the money issues by setting up direct debits for bills – leaving Callum money for food and fun. At least, he stopped buying so many DVDs and CDs from charity shops. Callum bought anything from the 1970s.

Callum's life changed again after Garry had his fatal accident as the farm had been passed on to him – not that he knew anything about it. Stefan had been contacted by Orkney Council on Callum's behalf after a law firm had traced Callum as the closest living relative. Stefan had a spark of inspiration. He contacted a social worker called Doug who he had been at college with and was working in Orkney. Between the two professionals, they negotiated a legal trust for Callum to retain ownership of the land until death, thereafter, it would be sold to the two workers who had looked after the farm for years.

It took a lot of time and co-operation from all the concerned parties, however, Callum was finally reconnected with his family's farm. The farm workers looked after Callum with kindness and gently introduced him into the community. It wasn't long before Callum became a well-known figure in the village. He was renowned for blasting out his sounds on the farm and for singing *Get It On* in the local pub karaoke every Saturday night. Callum seems to have found his true home in Orkney. He spends his days going for long walks, just listening to his music and blethering with the locals who have taken the big harmless soul to their hearts.

Zip

It's one thing having faith but another to believe that something you want to be true is true because you want it to be. People who are vulnerable, have a propensity to believe in such entities as faith healing, witchcraft, voodoo and magical powers. Two such people I know were Jean Wilson and her lifelong friend, June Marshall.

The two women met every week in Jean's house for a blether. Their relationship had changed since Jean had a life-changing accident which left her unable to walk without the aid of crutches. They used to have such a good social life and most of their discussions revolved around reminiscing about their former exploits. They talked for hours about lost weekends, hen parties (especially those Anne Summer's nights), ex-boyfriends, flat sharing and fun times. How things had changed. June saw herself as more of a relief carer for Jean's husband – giving him a break whilst she kept her pal company. Don't get me wrong, the women were still very fond of each other, but yearned that they could go back to the olden days before Jean's mobility had become restricted. Still, she was progressing slowly and had improved considerably from the initial impact of her injuries, caused when she fell off a horse, and her prognosis was good – just slow. June's problems were more domestic. Her son, Sam, aged seven, was being bullied and tormented at school. He had a terrible lisp and suffered from Tourette's. Consequently, she seemed to spend half her life up at his school trying to get him help, or being rebuked because of his behaviour. Sam reacted badly to the teasing he had to endure, and inevitably turned the air blue with bad language whenever he was stressed.

One Tuesday evening, the ladies were sitting in the living room, sharing a couple of bottles wine and a Chinese takeaway when there was a ping on June's phone – she glanced at the phone quickly. She saw a Facebook message appearing.

"Going to an event near you, guest speaker Zephinia Ilra Panacea, famous American faith healer, appearing at the Rila Spiritualist Church on Wednesday 1st April at 7:30. All welcome – free event but donations taken. Come along: seeing is believing."

The message was from Shirley, who was in their friend group. She wasn't really a friend but they both tagged her just to see what she was up to. After a drunken discussion on the merits and demerits of these inspirational speakers, they decided they would attend the event – after all, what harm could it do and maybe a bit of spirituality would do them good. They checked the preacher out on the Internet. Rev ZIP claimed he could cure all ills through the power given to him by a superpower. The testimonials on his site were incredible. Could this be the answer to their problems – maybe Jean could get back on her own two feet quicker and maybe Sam's lisp could be cured? Who knew?

The next night, Jean and June with young Sam in tow, turned up at the church early and sat in the front row, hoping to get picked by the rev. The preacher was introduced by Rose, a senior layperson. Rev ZIP started off with a solemn prayer and praised the Lord a lot of times. He carried on his oratory by describing the success he had with people in the States…He was impressive. He could fairly blow his own trumpet. There he stood, six-foot six-inches tall, impeccably dressed in an expensive looking suit and his deep, Texan tone drawled through to the excited audience:

"Do you believe, do you believe…" he must have bellowed fifty times as the crowd became more frenzied.

"I believe!" they chanted backed at him repeatedly.

"Does anyone here believe I can help them?" he inquired earnestly. A number of hands shot up immediately.

The first participant had all the makings of a ringer. A young, Black American teenager looking visibly upset was invited up to the stage.

"Oh! Honey! What is troubling you today?"

"I lost my phone, Reverend, with all my contact numbers on it. I am only here for a short vacation and I need that phone back. Can you help? Please?"

"What's your name, child?"

"Eve."

"Eve, write down your number right on this piece of paper – now don't show it to me!"

The preacher induced himself into a sort of trance. The crowd were stone silent as demanded. Suddenly, a ringtone was heard from the back of the room. He sent Eve to pick it up and much to her amazement, it was her phone.

"You are amazin'," she declared.

It could have been one of her friend's calling her but she didn't care – even it was a remarkable coincidence.

A moment later, the reverend called to the audience again.

"Who the heck is Alice? Is someone looking for Alice?"

A voice shrieked out:

"I am, she's my aunt who passed three months ago. I've been trying for a contact."

"You have one now! Alice is fine and at peace in heaven." The audience politely applauded the man.

Then Joseph, a local carpenter, was called up.

"Right, sir, what's your name?"

"What did you say?" said Joseph, adjusting his hearing aid.

"Hi, what's your name?" Zip enquired.

"Joseph – sorry, I'm deaf."

"How long you been wearing that hearing aid, Joe?"

"Since I've been deaf."

"Being told you were deaf must have been very difficult to hear?"

"Aye, it was – couldn't hear a thing."

"OK, mister, go behind that screen over there and wait till I call you."

Joe sallied over the stage and stood behind a big, white screen.

Next, he spotted our two protagonists waving furiously in the front row, trying to get noticed. He beckoned them to join him.

He asked Jean who she was and what had happened to her. She explained she was recovering slowly from a riding accident, but was desperate to walk without the crutches.

"Go behind that screen, Mrs Wilson, and pray!"

"OK, sonny, what's your name?"

"Them."

"How long has he had this affliction, Mum?"

"Since he could talk."

"Right on, Sam, go behind the screen with Mrs Wilson."

The Rev Zip urged the crowd to pray that his powers would work once more. There was a hush in the room as he began to speak.

He boomed, "Mrs Wilson, throw your crutches over the screen."

The first one came over, followed by the second. Then a clang.

He boomed again, "Samuel, say something!"

"Fuck. Mithuth Wilthsonth fell on her arth," Sam said.

Joseph had fallen asleep waiting to be called – he hadn't heard a thing.

The audience began to call out, "Cheat. Fraud!!!" They booed and hissed and other derogatory words were audible. The Rev ZIP was unabashed as he remonstrated with them as June went to the aid of her friend and her son.

"You did not believe enough, my friends," he kept repeating. He was ushered out of the building by a side door, his reputation tarnished.

After that fiasco, Jean resorted to the more traditional methods of recovery. She attended physiotherapy sessions and regained the power in her legs after a predicted time. June finally found a speech therapist who taught Sam to speak properly. He still swears like a trooper, but he does so politely.

The Rev ZIP lived up to his name that night by delivering ZIP. He continued to traverse across the small towns of America using their market stalls to pedal medicines to cure everything, baldness to xenophobia to gullible citizens believing the truth he spouts to them. The congregation resisted the temptation to invite any more American speakers to visit them again. The moral of the story is the old adage, 'If it sounds too good to be true, it usually is'.